Giles walked a few steps toward where Oz sat. "The material Valery sent me paints a rather disturbing picture of Koschei's evil tendencies."

"Yeah, but those are just stories, right?" Oz said. "Do we have any proof?"

Yaga turned her back on Faith, ignored Oz, and looked directly at Buffy and Giles. "I realize that you may not trust me, but you can trust this: The *Vozrozhdeniye* requires the life essence of many living souls to be sacrificed in order for the resurrection to occur. Many will die so Koschei can live. If you think that is not worth your time—"

"We do," Buffy said emphatically. Oz had raised a good point, though, and Buffy still didn't trust this woman as far as she could throw the lady's hut. "Giles, is that true?"

"Hm? Oh, yes, the *Vozrozhdeniye* does require death on a rather appalling scale."

"Fine." Buffy now looked back at Yaga. "How do we stop him?"

Buffy the Vampire Slayer™

Available from SIMON & SCHUSTER

The Deathless

Keith R. A. DeCandido

**An original novel based on the hit television series
created by Joss Whedon**

SIMON SPOTLIGHT ENTERTAINMENT
New York   London   Toronto   Sydney

This book is a work of fiction. Any references to historical events, real people, or real locales are used fictitiously. Other names, characters, places, and incidents are the product of the author's imagination, and any resemblance to actual events or locales or persons, living or dead, is entirely coincidental.

S|S|E

SIMON SPOTLIGHT ENTERTAINMENT

An imprint of Simon & Schuster Children's Publishing Division

1230 Avenue of the Americas, New York, New York 10020

™ & © 2006 Twentieth Century Fox Film Corporation. All rights reserved.

All rights reserved, including the right of reproduction in whole or in part in any form.

SIMON SPOTLIGHT ENTERTAINMENT and related logo are trademarks of Simon & Schuster, Inc.

Manufactured in the United States of America

First Edition 10 9 8 7 6 5 4 3 2 1

Library of Congress Control Number 2006933761

ISBN-13: 978-1-4169-3630-5

ISBN-10: 1-4169-3630-0

To Joseph Rosengaus—
he would've loved this book . . .

Acknowledgments

First off, thanks go to my wonderful editor Emily Westlake, who was the one who looked at the proposal for *The Deathless* and said, "Cool!" (she said more than that, actually, but that's what it boiled down to), and then did a fine job making the manuscript better, faster, and stronger. Thanks also to my agent, Lucienne Diver, for all the usual reasons, and probably some unusual ones as well; and to Patrick Price at SSE and Debbie Olshan at Fox, for all their kind and benevolent assistance.

Back in 1998, Marina Frants and I coauthored a short story called "A Bone to Pick" for *Did You Say Chicks!?* It was while working on that story, which also featured Baba Yaga, that I first got interested in Russian folklore, and without that interest, this book would never have happened, so mucho gratitude to Marina.

Several reference books were helpful, primary among them being *Russian Fairy Tales*, collected by Aleksandr Avanas'ev and translated into English by Norbert Guterman, and originally published in the United States in 1945.

Of course, I must thank Joss Whedon, the man who gave us *Buffy the Vampire Slayer* in the first place, as well as his cadre of writers for the show's third season, during which this novel takes place: the ever-delightful Jane Espenson, David Fury, David Greenwalt, Marti Noxon, Douglas Petrie, and Dan Vebber. I want to thank Vebber in particular, not only because he gave us two of the season's best episodes in "Lover's Walk" and "The Zeppo," but also because the latter provided me with the perfect placement for this book—to wit, right after it. ("The Zeppo" ends with both Willow and Giles being injured. They're fine by the time "Bad Girls" rolls around, and since neither is blessed with a Slayer's or a vampire's healing ability, it had to be at least a couple of weeks between episodes, which gave me enough room to tell a novel-size adventure.)

In addition, kudos to the actors who played the characters herein, who provided both face and voice for me to work with: Larry Bagby III (Larry), David Boreanaz (Angel), Nicholas Brendon (Xander), Charisma Carpenter (Cordelia), Justin Doran (Hogan), Eliza Dushku (Faith), Ethan Erickson (Percy), Sarah Michelle Gellar (Buffy), Seth Green (Oz), Saverio Guerra (Willy), Alyson Hannigan (Willow), Anthony Stewart Head (Giles), Keram Malicki-Sanchez (Freddy), Mercedes McNab (Harmony), Armin Shimerman (Snyder), Blake Soper (Michael), and Danny Strong (Jonathan).

The usual gangs of idiots: the Cross-Genre Abuse Group, my magnificent writers group, who had incredibly helpful suggestions; the Forebearance, in particular The Mom; *Kyoshi* Paul and the good folks at the dojo; all the wonderful people who were either involved with or attended the *Buffy* track at Dragon*Con 2005 and 2006; and the kind folks at the café who plied me with iced coffees and let me sit and work for as long as I wanted.

Finally, thanks to them that live with me, both human and feline, for everything.

Historian's Note

This novel takes place between the third season *Buffy the Vampire Slayer* episodes "The Zeppo" and "Bad Girls" (except where otherwise indicated).

Chapter One

Sunnydale, California, February 1999

"**D**o we *really* need to be just hangin' here, B?"

Buffy Summers's first instinct was to say something snide to her fellow Slayer, and a second later, she decided to give in to that instinct. After all, she was only talking about *Faith* here, and besides, she'd never been one to restrain herself from saying something snide. Outside of class, at least . . .

So she said, "Faith, any time you wanna book, feel free. It's just one vamp, I can probably handle it, even with one arm tied behind my back." She raised her right arm slightly, still in its sling after being strained during the fight against the Sisterhood of Jhe.

Defensively, Faith said, "You saying I can't?"

Suddenly wishing she'd ignored her first instinct, Buffy said, "No, Faith, I'm just saying that if you don't want to hang here, you can leave. Or not. I really don't care."

"Look at Little Miss Tight-ass. I was just askin', okay, B? Take a pill or something."

Rubbing the bridge of her nose with her good hand and closing her eyes in the vain hope of staving off a headache, Buffy said, "No, look—I'm sorry. I'm always a little testy after an apocalypse."

They were each sitting on a gravestone, the two on either end of a row of three, all of which had the name TOOMAJIAN carved into them. The stones Buffy and Faith sat on had been there for a while. The one between them was shiny and new, its occupant having died only within the last week. They'd been sitting there, in the midst of one of Sunnydale's dozen cemeteries, for the better part of half an hour, waiting for the inevitable. This one was the Restwell Cemetery, distinguished by the fact that there were no mausoleums. All the gravestones had a religious symbol carved into the gravestones above the name—crosses, Stars of David, what have you—and said graves were laid out in a strict linear pattern.

And how sad is it that I know all the cemeteries in town this *well?*

Shaking her head, Faith said, "Least you're alive to *be* testy. Beats the crap outta the alternative."

"True," Buffy said with a sigh.

Faith pulled one leg up so that her foot was resting on the edge of the grave, her knee near her chin. "I'll stick around, I guess. I mean, between the two of us, we make one whole Slayer, right?"

Buffy smiled, her gaze trailing back down to the sling, which was supposed to come off tomorrow. Not a moment too soon, as far as Buffy was concerned, but Dr. Klesaris had been pretty insistent that it stay on until then. As it was, the doc was stunned at how fast she was healing. Of course, Buffy couldn't tell Klesaris that she was the Slayer, the chosen one, the girl granted the power and ability to fight creatures of the night. She healed fast.

Or, rather, she thought, *I'm one of the chosen two.* When one Slayer died, a new one was activated, but whoever started the Slayer ball rolling millennia ago didn't account for CPR. When Buffy had died facing the Master, a new Slayer was called—but then Xander Harris had been able to revive Buffy with the "breath of life." Result: two Slayers for the price of one.

Right now, though, Faith's line about the two of them making one whole Slayer wasn't entirely a joke. Looking over at the other grave, Buffy saw that Faith's black eye had finally healed, but she had a cast on her right wrist—amusingly, a mirror image of the one on Giles's left—and Buffy had been able to tell from the way Faith walked that her cracked ribs weren't a hundred percent yet, either. It had been a brutal fight against the creatures that the Sisterhood of Jhe called forth from the Hellmouth, and it had taken a supreme effort from Buffy, Faith, and Angel on the physical side and Giles and Willow on the magical to avert the end of the world.

Indicating Buffy's sling with her head, Faith asked, "So when you getting that thing off?"

"Tomorrow. The day of the stupid assembly."

Faith grinned. "You mean there are assemblies that *aren't* stupid?"

"Good point. Buffy scores one for redundancy."

"What's the occasion?"

"Ring Day approacheth. When all Sunnydale High students show their school spirit by wearing ugly jewelry on their right hand."

Giving Buffy the same look she'd give soup she found a fly in, Faith said, "You're not going for that, are you, B?"

"That would be a big no. Leaving aside the whole lack-of-school-spirit issue, Mom really can't afford it."

"No loss, you ask me. Course, I'm not exactly the poster girl for stayin' in school, huh?" Faith looked down at the grave between them. "You sure this lady'll be a vamp?"

Shrugging, Buffy said, "Willow hacked the autopsy report—said Katherine Toomajian died with puncture wounds on her neck and blood in her mouth that wasn't hers. That's pretty much textbook for 'vamp in waiting.'"

Faith made a show of looking at the nonexistent watch on her wrist. "Well, time's a-wastin' here, B. I'm not sayin' you're wrong, but we've been sittin' here for a good while, and—"

Buffy hopped down off the marker for Katherine's father. "No, you're right, it's getting la—"

Then something caught her eye. She'd been staring

down at the loose dirt in front of Katherine Tooma-jian's grave for thirty minutes from the vantage point of the grave next to it. It wasn't until she looked at it from this new angle that she noticed the splinter of wood.

"What is it, B?"

Getting down on one knee, Buffy started digging with the only fingers she was able to move freely. "Faith, give me a hand here—and yes, I mean that literally."

Faith did so, lending her left hand to aid Buffy's. "What's up?"

But before Buffy could answer, they unearthed two more splinters, both a bit bigger than the first.

They exchanged a glance. Buffy said, "The coffin's been broken. She's already out."

That was when they heard the scream.

Moving as one, the two Slayers straightened and started running toward the noise—or, rather, what they each thought was the noise. "Faith, it's *this* way!" Buffy yelled even as she continued toward the main entrance.

Faith, however, said, "It's back this way, B!"

Buffy considered following Faith, then decided her fellow Slayer was an idiot. The voice was *definitely* coming from the main entrance. Besides, even if Buffy were wrong, it was a lot easier to get out through the main entrance than to hop the fence when you've only got one working arm.

Then she heard the scream again—coming from the street, about at the spot toward which Faith was running.

Crap. I hate it when she's right.

She kept moving toward the entrance anyhow, because while Faith was right about the scream, Buffy was right about it being much easier to hit the street through the egress.

The main gate was open. When Buffy had first moved to Sunnydale, Restwell Cemetery locked the gate after ten in the evening, but after the twentieth time some vampire (or, occasionally, some Slayer) broke the lock, they gave up and just left it open, figuring that would be cheaper than constantly buying new padlocks and chains.

Buffy immediately turned down Arisztid Avenue—which appeared deserted, unsurprisingly. Most Sunnydale residents knew better than to be wandering the streets near the cemeteries at night.

But there's always one idiot who insists on being bloodsucker breakfast.

Turning the corner onto Blasko Street, Buffy saw a vampire throwing a young man to the sidewalk. The vampire was covered in dirt and had her game face on, but Buffy still was able to recognize the long, straight brown hair, full lips, and general height and build as being that of Katherine Toomajian, mugging victim, based on the files Willow had hacked into.

"I'm impressed. Usually vamps don't have the brains to smooth out the dirt after they crawl out."

Buffy heard a clang, and both she and Katherine turned toward the fence to see Faith trying—and failing—to climb it one-handed.

Katherine broke into a wide, fang-laden grin.

"Both Slayers. Excellent. I'd have settled for one of you."

That threw Buffy for a loop. "You know about us?" Most newly minted vamps hadn't gotten a chance to look at the instruction manual.

"I've been studying you for *years*. Took me forever to find a night-dweller who would immortalize me."

Rolling her eyes, Buffy said, "Great, another wannabe. You're not immortal, you're just dead. Well, mostly dead." She pulled out her stake. "And you're about to become all dead."

Katherine responded by growling, picking her intended victim up, and tossing him into the fence, which startled Faith, who had abandoned climbing and was now attempting to make it to the top of the wrought-iron fence with a single jump.

"I've been waiting for this moment for years, Slayer. What better way to prove my worth to my fellow night-dwellers than to—"

She was interrupted by a jumping side kick that Buffy delivered to her solar plexus. Both Slayer and vampire fell to the sidewalk, but Buffy was able to roll on her good shoulder and quickly stand up. Katherine was still sprawled on the sidewalk, and looked kind of put out that Buffy hadn't let her finish her speech.

Buffy lunged forward with her stake, intending to sink it into Katherine's heart, but the vampire was able to roll to her left and out of the way, simultaneously delivering a roundhouse kick to Buffy's right shoulder.

Knives of pain sliced through Buffy's entire right side—that part of her body was still tender from her encounter with the occupants of the Hellmouth—and it distracted her long enough for Katherine to get to her feet.

Out of the corner of her eye Buffy saw Faith take a dozen steps back and then start running toward the fence in order to take another shot at jumping it. Buffy immediately went on the offensive, not wanting Katherine to see that another Slayer was likely about to join the fight.

Katherine's intended victim had run off, and was now long gone. *More power to you, buddy,* Buffy thought, *and next time, wait till morning to get that pack of smokes or whatever.* Buffy wasn't sure what reason the guy'd had for being out at night, but she'd discovered in the years since she was called to Slayer-tude that it was usually for a dumb reason like that, with people thinking, *Well, nothing bad could possibly happen to* me*!*

Normally Buffy attacked with a combination of kicks and punches, but she emphasized the former now for obvious reasons. She went after Katherine with a left front snap kick, followed by a right roundhouse kick to her stomach and then another to her head. The idea was to distract her with the first two, leaving her open for the third.

Unfortunately, Katherine wasn't encumbered by a nonfunctioning wing, and she was able to block all three kicks, then follow up with a haymaker that caught Buffy right in the jaw. The blow wasn't hard enough to bring her down, but she fell to her knees anyhow, hoping to lull Katherine into a false sense of security.

"I've got you now, Slayer."

Then the vamp looked up, hearing the whooshing sound of a person jumping through the air but unable to react before Faith landed on her. Buffy smiled; Faith had leapt up high enough to brace herself with her one good hand on the top of the fence, flip over, and land right on Katherine's dirt-covered head.

Still, the attack had more surprise to it than power, since Faith had only been able to use one hand to flip. Katherine got to her feet quickly, only to find herself facing two Slayers.

"Maybe you'd have settled for one," Buffy said, "but now you've got two."

Katherine looked at Buffy, looked at Faith, looked at Buffy again, and then turned and ran away down Blasko.

It took Buffy and Faith a moment to realize what was happening. They exchanged a quick "What the *hell*?" glance and then motored after her, Buffy shoving her stake back in her jacket's inner pocket.

Faith called after their prey, "For someone who's so hot to bag two Slayers, you sure turn tail quick, bitch!"

For her part, Buffy just focused on running. She was in her usual patrol gear, which emphasized comfort over fashion—not that she ever completely abandoned fashion, as she wore a black Roxy T-shirt and a black pair of Seven jeans. Both were purchased during a shopping spree on Rodeo Drive two summers ago with her indulgent and long-suffering dad. In deference to the nippy February weather, she wore her black knee-length coat. And, of course, she had on Nikes. She was perfectly capable of running in heels, but it wasn't something she'd go out of her way to do on purpose.

Buffy and Faith had spent a lot of time training together since Faith first arrived in Sunnydale last fall, and Buffy was now amused to see that the two of them were keeping almost perfect pace with each other. The problem was, they weren't keeping pace with Katherine, who was pulling farther and farther ahead.

"Let's get the lead out, B," Faith said through clenched teeth, and the brunette suddenly zoomed past Buffy.

Oh no you don't. Buffy took a deep breath, the cool night air searing her lungs, and started pumping her own legs faster.

Blasko ended at Guterman Drive, and Katherine made the turn at full speed. Buffy ran a few steps behind Faith in the same direction.

At the corner of Guterman and Palombo Court, the vampire suddenly stopped and cringed, hissing and holding up her arms as if trying to ward something off.

Faith was a few steps ahead, so she got to her first, but Katherine flailed with one arm and knocked her to the side.

"Get me away! Get me away from her!" Katherine was practically screeching.

Buffy ran up to her. The vampire smelled like fresh dirt and worms, the same as most vamps did when they first crawled from their graves. Buffy also detected the faint ammonia-like tinge of disinfectant. Or maybe it was embalming fluid. That was something Buffy tried not to think too hard about.

"Now you're asking for *help*?" Buffy asked. "Don't make me laugh." She then kicked Katherine in the face, punctuated with a "Ha!" Another kick, another "Ha!" Then a third time, with yet another "Ha!"

"Look at that," Buffy said, "you made me laugh, after I told you not to." She pulled the stake out of her pocket.

Katherine let loose with a sweeping kick of her own, which Buffy avoided with a leap. The vampire was still cowering, but also not moving. Buffy tried to attack again, but this time Katherine was able to bat her aside the way she did Faith.

Faith, however, had had time to get up, and she started punching Katherine with both hands—which Buffy thought couldn't have been good for her healing right wrist. Still, Faith managed to knock the vampire all the way down to the sidewalk. Katherine flailed again, knocking Faith aside, but that just gave Buffy an opening to thrust her stake into the vampire's chest.

"No, it's not supposed to end like—" Again, Katherine was cut off, this time by her larynx—and the rest of her—turning into a fine powder. Just like that, the dirt-and-ammonia smell was replaced by the whiff of moldy dust that characterized a vampire's death.

Then nothing. Just the semiclean night air of suburban SoCal.

"That was messed up," Faith said as she clambered to her feet.

"Yeah," Buffy said. "One minute she's all, 'I'm gonna get you, Slaya,' then she's all shaken *and* stirred."

She looked up at the house on the corner, which looked like every other split-level in Sunnydale, with the usual slanted tile roof and dull aluminum siding. Nobody got architectural awards designing houses in this town. This particular place had a small lawn in front, a driveway on the Palombo Court side, and a large yard between it and the next house down that looked like it stretched around to the back. Across Guterman was a large municipal parking lot. *So unless the late Ms. Toomajian had a fear of parking lots, it was this house that got her wigged.*

Faith shook her head. "I've never seen a vamp act like that when sunlight or holy water wasn't involved."

"I have." Buffy found her gaze drawn back to the split-level as she remembered an incident from shortly after her arrival in Sunnydale. "Couple years ago now," she added for Faith's benefit. "And it was a house a lot like this that had a vampire doing the quaky knees thing."

"Who lived in the house?"

"A praying mantis. It almost ate Xander alive."

"Really?" Faith said that with an almost feral smile.

Before Buffy could ask what the other Slayer was thinking, her right shoulder started throbbing like a bass drum. "Ouchie, ouchie."

"Yeah, I know what you mean," Faith said, holding up her right arm and clenching her fingers into as tight a fist as the cast would allow. "My wrist is givin' me grief too. Wanna call it a night?"

"Just one thing." Buffy walked over to the mailbox that sat at the edge of the front lawn to check the name.

Taped to the side was a piece of paper, on which was written, in rather neat handwriting, the name Y. DRYANUSHKINA.

Hope I can remember that. Buffy couldn't write well with the sling, and besides, she hadn't brought a piece of paper or pencil with her. She didn't even bother to ask Faith if she had.

Then she looked up. *Duh, I've got the address. And I think I can remember 123 Guterman Drive.*

"I'll have Willow dig into this tomorrow," Buffy said. "For now, I see a very, very hot bath in my immediate future."

"I hear that, B," Faith said with a ragged smile. Buffy suspected her wrist was hurting more than she would let on.

I just hope it's not another praying mantis. . . .

Chapter Two

"If you'll just sign here, Mr. Gills, we'll be on our way."

Rupert Giles took the proffered clipboard from the contractor with his injured left hand, heartened to see that his fractured left arm had healed enough that he could grip things again. As he removed the pen from underneath the clip, he said to the burly man in the gray outfit—the name tag on the breast of which said *BRACKEN*—"It's Giles, actually."

"Whatever." Bracken rolled his eyes while scratching his shaved head with a meaty finger.

Somehow, Giles restrained himself from sighing through his teeth as he signed the work order on the proverbial dotted line. Besides, what Mr. Bracken and his cohorts lacked in the ability to pronounce names they made up for in job skills. The thankfully brief opening of the Hellmouth had left the Sunnydale High School Library in a bit of a shambles, but Mr. Bracken's people had just this morning finished their work in restoring the library to its former state.

Handing the clipboard back, Giles said, "Thank you very much, Mr. Brackish."

"No problem. Have a nice day." With that insincerity out of the way, Mr. Bracken tore off one copy of the form, handed it back to Giles, stuck the clipboard in a duffle bag, which he then slung over his shoulder, and exited the library.

Giles was grateful that the work had been done at all. Principal Snyder had wanted to just rope off the part of the floor that was damaged and pay only to have someone clean out the muck. It had taken a certain amount of convincing on Giles's part to get the principal to reverse that position—an hour of his life he was certain he'd want back when he was on his deathbed. Thankfully, Giles had already been put on painkillers, which allowed him to stave off the headache that encounters with Snyder always gave him.

The clincher had been when Giles was able (with Willow's help) to ascertain that the school had taken out an insurance claim. "Vandals high on PCP" was what Snyder had put as the cause of the damage, and Giles was of the opinion that the resultant monetary reward should be put into actually fixing the damage in question. This opinion was reinforced by the threat of a call to an agent at the insurance company, who wasn't likely to take well to the payout going into something other than the repairs they were specifically earmarked for, according to the policy.

Now, though, it was all finished. The floor and bookcases were replaced, the cage and main desk repaired, and all was right with the world.

Giles sat down and started sorting through the mail that he'd picked up in the main office earlier. Among the envelopes was a somewhat battered box with an air bill that indicated it had been shipped from Valery Kochevikov, a Russian folklorist. Intrigued, Giles tore the package open.

The box contained several items, including a few charts, a scroll, a massive book, and a letter. Assuming the letter to contain the gist of why Valery felt the need to send Giles the rest of it, he began to peruse it.

When he was done, he found himself saying the two words he hoped in vain he would be able to go a day without ever saying: "Oh, dear."

"Why, Giles, I didn't know you cared. I think you're a dear too," Buffy said.

Looking up, the erstwhile Watcher saw Buffy and Willow entering. Glancing up at the clock on the wall as he put Valery's letter down on the table with the rest of the items, Giles registered that it was still fifteen minutes before homeroom. Buffy no longer had her arm in a sling, which was in keeping with her physician's instructions. As for Willow, the swelling on her left cheek had gone down almost completely. "Good morning, Buffy. Good morning, Willow."

Willow looked around. "The construction's all done!"

"Yes, the contractors just left."

Buffy nodded. "Good job. The place looks boring as new."

"Indeed." Giles pulled out his handkerchief with one hand, removed his spectacles with the other, and started cleaning them rather than castigating Buffy. He was hardly about to take decorating advice from an American teenager. He saw the clothes she chose to decorate herself with every day, after all. "How was patrol last night?"

Buffy fell more than sat in one of the chairs that surrounded the main table, placing her books in front of her. "We came, we saw, we staked. Katherine Toomajian is now dirt on the Guterman Drive sidewalk."

Frowning, Giles said, "Guterman is several blocks from the cemetery where Ms. Toomajian was interred."

"She pulled a Count Rugen on us, and we chased her down the streets. We only caught up to her because she went all cringe-y at some house."

"What house?" Giles asked.

"Just your ordinary suburban split-level, decorated in early high dull. But this vamp freaked out the exact same way as the vampire who went crazy at Ms. French's house."

He put his glasses back on. "You fear there is another praying mantis?"

"That's the working theory."

Willow added, "And I'll be using the ol' computer skills to see how well it works."

"Very good."

Buffy peered down at the contents of Valery's package. "So what's the special delivery?"

"Oh, it's, ah, from an old friend—Valery Kochevikov. He's a prominent Russian folklorist, as far as the general public is concerned."

Willow, who now sat next to Buffy, grinned. "And by night he's a superexpert on the occult?"

"Well, he is one of the foremost authorities on Eastern European mysticism, yes." He picked up Valery's letter. "According to him, some time in the next week or so, the stars will be properly aligned for an attempt to perform the *Vozrozhdeniye* on Koschei the Deathless."

"Wait! I know that name!" Willow shook her arm up and down and scrunched up her face. "Don't tell me. . . ." Suddenly Willow's eyes widened, her entire face brightening. "*I* know! You said Russian folklore— Koschei the Deathless is from Russian fairy tales, right?"

Nodding approvingly, Giles said, "Yes, Willow, very good."

"During that whole Hansel-and-Gretl thing last month I did a lot of reading on fairy tales while I was grounded. The Russian ones are fun. There's Prince Ivan and Bulat the Brave and Vasilisa the Wise and Baba Yaga—and Koschei."

Giles shuddered, but he was grateful for Willow's eternal optimism. The "Hansel-and-Gretl thing" she discussed so casually was an event that had almost gotten Willow killed—by her own mother's hand. Several Sunnydale parents were magically influenced by a demon posing as two dead children. The demon had done this before, and had been the basis for the stories about Hansel and Gretl. Buffy was able to stop it—though not before one of Willow's fellow students of magic, Amy, was turned into a rat. Attempts to turn her back into a human had thus far proven unsuccessful.

Buffy looked up at Giles. "So someone wants to perform the Voice of Nay on this Koschei person?"

With a long-suffering sigh, Giles corrected her. "*Vozrozhdeniye*. It's a resurrection spell that can revive a dead wizard by using the life force of other people."

Willow frowned. "I've never heard of that ritual."

Sternly, Giles said, "As well you shouldn't. The *Vozrozhdeniye* is necromancy—death magic."

Both girls' faces wrinkled up. "Can I get an *ew-men*?" Buffy muttered.

"Yeah. Ick." Willow added. "No thanks. I'll stick to levitating pencils and driving back demons."

"Good call, Will." Buffy then asked Giles, "So who's this Koschei guy?"

Giles removed his glasses and started pacing. "Koschei was a sorcerer in Russia a few hundred years ago. He was quite powerful, though he mostly kept to himself. Most of the tales that Willow likely read involve people tricking him or trying to rescue people he kidnapped, but Valery's research indicates that the only parts of those tales that correspond to reality are the ones where he kidnapped people. Rarely did they return alive. He gained the nickname 'the Deathless' because he could not die."

"So what happened?" Willow asked.

"He died." Giles put his glasses back on.

"O-o-o-o-kay," Buffy said.

Giles walked over to the table and flipped the large book open to a woodcut illustration of a person astride a horse. A helmet with large round eyeholes covered the top of his head, and the bottom was obscured by a long, waist-length beard. The person carried both a shield and a staff, the latter topped off by a star. "That is one of the illustrations of Koschei. Valery isn't sure how he met his end—some say that the Prince Ivan who Willow mentioned did it—but the important thing is that he may be resurrected. The Hellmouth is an ideal locale to attempt the"—he smirked slightly—"'Voice of Nay.'"

Buffy turned to look at Willow. "Write this day down, Will—Giles made a funny."

In a mock-conspiratorial tone, Willow said, "See, take him out of the Watchers and he almost becomes a regular guy."

"Emphasis, of course, on almost."

"If you're quite finished," Giles said in a stern tone, though he had to admit to enjoying the repartée. And perhaps there was some truth to Willow's statement. He was no longer officially a Watcher. Buffy still treated him as such, for which he was grateful—after the betrayal of trust that was inherent to the Cruciamentum, Giles wasn't sure he'd even get her respect back—but their relationship had altered. Into what, Giles wasn't sure yet. He was curious as to how things would further change once the new Watcher arrived.

As if she had read his mind, Buffy asked, "Speaking of which, any word when Giles Mark II's showing up?"

"Not yet. After the unpleasantness with Mrs. Post, the Council is being a bit more careful."

"Tell them to take their time. Or better yet, tell them not to bother. I've already got a perfectly good Watcher."

Giles looked down and tried not to smile too widely. "Thank you," he said softly, then added in a louder tone: "In any event, we should be vigilant. Valery has outlined the indicators for which we must be on the lookout. The first is the theft of a dead body, specifically that of a man who died with no damage to his face."

"That's not a problem," Willow said. "I've already got the coroner bookmarked."

"Indeed." Giles recalled that her perusal of death investigations was what had led Buffy and Faith to their kill last night. "In the meantime I will read over Valery's papers and see what else we will need to know."

The Klaxon that indicated homeroom was about to start echoed throughout Sunnydale High School's halls.

"Another day, another duller," Buffy said, getting up and grabbing her books. "Will, can you check into—" She blinked. "Hey, I just realized. The woman who owned the house where the vamp went kooky last night—her last name was Drya-something. It was definitely Russian. Or Russian-ish, anyhow." She snapped her fingers. "Dryanushkina, that's it!"

Frowning, Giles said, "It *could* be a coincidence."

"How many times, Giles? I don't believe in coincidences or leprechauns."

Again, Giles smirked. "So you keep insisting—and the point is well taken."

Willow said, "Don't worry—I'll dig into this Dryanushkina lady and see why she makes creatures that go bump in the night go bump in the night."

"Excellent," Giles said. "However, for now it would be best if you weren't *too* late for homeroom."

"Away we go," Buffy said, and she and Willow departed.

For his part, Giles sat at the table and began reading Valery's material in depth. Necromancy was nasty business—even during Giles's misspent youth, he and his mates had never gotten into death magic. He was particularly grateful that Willow had such an aversion to it. The young girl had only been studying magic for a year, and she was clearly quite good at it. Her potential was theoretically limitless. *She will bear watching.*

That caused him to wince, for he was no longer officially a Watcher. *But that hardly matters. I have a responsibility to Buffy and to Faith—and to Willow, to Xander, to Oz, even, God help me, to Cordelia. Whether or not I draw a salary from a bunch of pillocks locked in their bloody castle in England is irrelevant.*

Having reassured himself that he wasn't wasting his time on duties that would soon be assumed by whoever the Council saw fit to send along, Giles continued reading Valery's material.

• • •

Buffy struggled to stay awake through the school day. It started with an irritating European History class. Every time Europe was mentioned to her lately, she thought about the Watchers' Council. Their little eighteenth-birthday present was bad enough, but that they made Giles do it for them was worse, and worse even than that was their incompetence resulted in Buffy's mother being put in harm's way.

After that was an English class that might have been more compelling if Buffy had actually read the Wordsworth poem under discussion, and a math class that bore a more-than-passing resemblance to gibberish. Buffy generally did fine at math, but Mr. Liegey was quite simply the world's most boring human, and he managed to make every problem look impossible and ridiculous.

After that, though, she was free. The next two periods were lunch and study hall, both of which could be spent in the library, and the classes after that were canceled for seniors, so they could go to the stupid Ring Day assembly.

Buffy and Willow headed from math to their lockers to drop off their books, then intended to go libraryward for quality research time. Buffy wanted to know what the deal was with this Russian woman who showed up right when someone from Russia was warning Giles about the resurrection of a Russian sorcerer. They needed to be rushin' to find out what was going on.

Oh, God, I've been hanging around Xander way too long. . . .

Oz joined the girls as they were depositing schoolbooks into their respective lockers. Next to them, J. D. Brodsky and Maria DeMatteo were gabbing.

"So, you gettin' a ring?"

"Duh! You think I wasted four years of my life to *not* get a ring?"

"I heard Jonathan wasn't gettin' one."

"Yeah, but Jonathan, like, *wallows* in lameness. His loserdom is well documented, so of *course* he isn't getting one."

J. D. and Maria walked off. Buffy sighed and had to restrain herself from slamming her locker shut. Last time she did that, she broke it, and then had to listen to Snyder harangue her about damaging school equipment. The locker still didn't close right.

Willow had her sad face on. "I'm sorry, Buffy. If it makes you feel any better, *I* don't think you're a loser."

"That makes one of you."

Buffy looked up to see Cordelia approaching.

"Let me guess," Cordy went on, "none of you are getting a ring?"

Willow suddenly brightened. "I am! I think I'm gonna get a silver one. See, then I can use it to help with spells, 'cause you can channel magic with silver. You can't do that with gold. Besides, you know, there's the whole 'cheaper' thing."

Oz shrugged. "I had the chance last year, but it throws off the strumming. Besides, Ring Day's Monday."

At first Buffy was confused, then she remembered that Monday was the night after the next full moon. The Ring Day ceremony began after school, and, since it was February, it was likely to get dark before it was all over. Having one of the seniors turn into a werewolf in the middle of the ceremony was probably high on Snyder's list of things he didn't want happening, and getting stampeded or shot five minutes later was probably high on Oz's.

Cordelia flashed her best I'm-so-much-better-than-you smile. "Well, it's nothing but eighteen karats for *this* girl."

With that, she walked off.

Oz regarded her retreating form. "She does know how to darken up a room, doesn't she?"

Willow had gone back to sad face mode. "I'm sorry you can't get one."

"It's no big," Buffy said, even though it was. "Mom just can't afford it. The gallery's not doing as well as she'd like this year, and the cost of the repairs for the house after my welcome-home party was pretty steep."

They started walking down the hall toward the library, only to see Xander zipping toward them. "Hey, Xander," Buffy said.

"Hi Buff, hi Will, hi Oz. Gotta go."

"Where's the fire?"

"No fire, just have some things to take care of." He gave a thumbs-up. "Gotta be ready for Ring Day, am I right?"

"You're getting a ring?" Willow asked, sounding surprised.

"Of course! You won't be seeing Xander Harris lumped in with the losers and the ne'er-do-wells and the people who get made fun of. Those days are in the past, my good friends. And with that, I go."

Xander turned and walked briskly down the hall.

Willow gazed after him. "He's been acting strange ever since he started driving his uncle's car. And I'm surprised he's getting a ring. His parents don't usually pay for that kind of thing, and it's not like Xander can afford it himself."

Buffy let out a breath. "A problem for a time that is other. For now, it's on with the research."

Nodding, Willow said, "Right." Now it was the infamous resolved face, and all three of them proceeded to the library.

"Okay, this is weird."

At the time of Willow's rather disturbing pronouncement Buffy was idly flipping through the pile of woodcut illustrations that that Russian guy had sent Giles by way of avoiding math homework. The librarian himself was at the main desk, performing that rarest of duties, aiding a student who needed a book for a class.

Buffy got up and stood behind Willow, who sat at the table squinting at her laptop.

"I really don't like the sound of 'weird,'" Buffy said.

Oz was sitting next to Willow and added, "Well, it's a relative term."

"Right now," Willow said, "we're still in 'I'm confused' weird, not 'This is going to strangle us in our sleep' weird." She pointed at the Internet browser screen she had up. "I only found one Dryanushkina, and her first name's Yulia."

"Perfect," Buffy said with a nod.

Pointing at the laptop screen, Willow said, "That's her driver's license."

Buffy peered at the screen. "Right address, too. 123 Guterman. So far, so good."

"That's not the weird part." Willow maximized another window with the mouse, which overlaid the previous one. It showed a newspaper article discussing the abandoning of a construction project on Guterman Drive.

Reading aloud from the article, Buffy said, "'The Clancy Construction Company has announced that all work has ceased on the 123 Condominium Project, which was to be constructed at that address on Guterman Drive on a lot that has been abandoned for over thirty years.'" Buffy looked at the date of the article. "This is from two months ago."

"And note the picture," Oz said.

Buffy did so. It was a long view of a vacant lot, big enough to show the house that had been to the left of the Dryanushkina residence, as well as the corner of Palombo Court.

"I'm not exactly an expert," Oz said, "but doesn't it take longer than two months to build a split-level?"

"Not to mention seed an entire yard." Buffy pointed at the picture, specifically the dirt that made up most of the vacant lot. "Our lady's house had a manicured lawn. In fact, that lawn had a pedicure and a facial."

Willow frowned. "Buffy, you said the house looked like every other house in town, right?"

"Yeah, right out of *Sunnydale Homes and Gardens*. Why?"

"A good illusion spell will show what the viewer expects to see."

Giles, who had finished with the student and had been listening in, wandered over. "Willow is correct. The most likely explanation for the disparity between what you and Faith saw last night and those photographs from two months ago is a very sophisticated illusion spell."

Buffy gave Giles a look. "I got that from what Willow said, and she used a lot fewer words."

"Er, yes." Giles took off his glasses and started wiping them. "In any case, I think it would be best if you investigated that house—or lot, or whatever it might be—in daylight."

"Then to Guterman Drive we shall go." Buffy then let out a very long sigh. "After Snyder's assembly."

"I believe the assembly has something to do with the ring ceremony," Giles said.

"As far as I'm concerned, it's an excuse to miss Chemistry and Spanish. All else is gravy."

"Buffy?"

Turning to Willow, the Slayer said, "Yeah, Will?"

Willow had her ooh-ick face on. "I just checked— Yulia Dryanushkina's a retired substitute teacher. Just like Ms. French was."

Closing her eyes, Buffy exhaled slowly through her teeth, then walked over to the cage.

Giles looked confused. "Buffy, what are you—"

"I'm getting a machete, Giles. It's another praying mantis, I'm *sure* of it."

Chapter Three

"As you all know, Ring Day is rapidly approaching. That means it's time for all seniors—or, at least, all seniors who have a modicum of school spirit—to purchase your unique, one-of-a-kind Class of 1999 rings, just like every class before you did. For those of you who don't know what the word 'modicum' means, I suggest you find a dictionary, hand it to a friend—assuming you have one—and tell them to hit you over the head with it."

Buffy had spent most of Principal Snyder's speech up until this point making an in-depth study of the fingernail on her left index finger. With the sling, she hadn't gotten much of a look at her nails lately, so she enjoyed studying them now that the brace was a sling of the past.

At least the assembly was in the school auditorium. She had lived in fear of his having it in the gym, which would have meant sitting on the wooden bleachers doing the butt-ache shuffle for an hour. Luckily, since the assembly was only for a quarter of the school's population, he held it here in the auditorium, filled with comfortable seats complete with backs and armrests.

By the time he'd gotten to the dictionary line, she'd moved on to the next finger, and debated brandishing it at the principal. But, no, that would just put her back on his radar. Snyder had had it in for Buffy from day one, and had even expelled her before her mother and Giles had gone over his beady little head to the California state authorities. Even so, he had made it his personal mission to make her life as miserable as possible.

So she did what she always did when Snyder was driving her crazy—in this case, by boring her to tears with a speech about the acquisition of a ring she was not getting: She remembered the band candy. Giles's old rival Ethan Rayne had done a magical whammy on some candy that regressed all the adults who ate it into their teenage selves. In Snyder's case, it confirmed everything Buffy had dreamed was the case: As a kid, Snyder was the twerpy guy who always tagged along even though nobody wanted him around. That he grew into the embittered little creep they had all learned to despise came as no shock.

Snyder droned on. He was now extolling the virtues of a school spirit that he himself had done more to crush in the last two years than any number of unexplained deaths.

"Your class ring isn't just another piece of jewelry for you to wear with your necklaces and other rings and bracelets and strange piercings, and whatever other vile and depraved things you kids do to your bodies in the name of fashion. A ring is a symbol—a symbol of unity, and a symbol of cooperation, and a symbol of spirit. It shows that you attend this school, and that you're proud to do so. And let me remind you that it isn't just something you wear because it matches your outfit. The school ring is there to match your soul—assuming any of you kids *have* a soul, a fact I'm more than a little skeptical of."

Buffy looked around to see where Xander was sitting. She, Willow, and Oz had been late to the assembly, and therefore had taken the first three seats available. Buffy saw Cordelia, sitting with Harmony and a bunch of other Cordettes, and most of the rest of the senior class, but of Xander, there was no sign. *That's odd. And dangerous—Snyder doesn't take well to people who avoid his rants.*

Certainly, he was deep into rant mode. "And furthermore—get that gum out of your mouth, mister!—*not* wearing a ring will serve only to prove what I've always believed: that you're a useless collection of malcontents, ne'er-do-wells, and imbeciles who can eagerly look forward to a career of asking people if they want fries to go with their burgers."

Buffy found herself with an image of Snyder, his ears sticking out from under the silly yellow cap of a Doublemeat Palace uniform, asking if he could take her order. It took all of Buffy's self-control to keep from giggling. She did grin, though, and that caused Willow to grin and then hit Buffy playfully on the arm, mouthing the words, *Stop that!*

After a few more eternities, Snyder finally said, "All right, that's it. For those of you who haven't signed up for your ring, today's the last day. Sign-up sheets are outside the auditorium. The Ring Day ceremony will be Monday after school. Anyone who has signed up for a ring but does not attend will neither get their ring nor have their money refunded, unless they have a note from a doctor. And by that I mean a real doctor, with a diploma and everything— I do intend to check—and also make sure that it's a doctor who actually practices in the State of California, and is still alive. Yes, Brodsky, I'm looking at you."

Buffy was grateful he said that, since it appeared as if Snyder were looking directly at her. Instead, it was at J. D., who was right behind her. Glancing back, she saw him sinking slowly into his seat. Maria was next to him, giggling.

"All right, that's it. See you all tomorrow—*after* I see you at the sign-up table outside."

Before Snyder had finished that sentence most of the seniors had risen from their seats and were practically stepping over each other to reach the exit.

"Have you seen Xander?" Willow asked as they joined the slow-moving queue of students jammed next to each other in the narrow aisle.

Shaking her head, Buffy said, "Nope. I hope Snyder didn't notice."

"I wish I knew what was happening with him. I think it's that car."

That was the second time Willow had blamed Xander's behavior on the convertible his uncle Rory had lent him. Xander had started driving it recently—right before that craziness with the Sisterhood of Jhe—and he *had* been acting a little strange since then.

In the throng of people Buffy soon found herself separated from Willow and Oz. Eventually, she made it through the doors, at which point everyone scattered to the nine winds, freeing up movement considerably. Most went down one of the hallways. Several went to the sign-up table—in fact, Larry Blaisdell almost stepped on Jonathan Levinson as they both approached. Considering Jonathan could comfortably fit inside one of Larry's forearms . . .

Buffy started looking around for her fellow Scoobies. They were going to take Oz's van over to Guterman to check out the house belonging to the woman Buffy was morally certain was another praying mantis.

God, I hope Xander hasn't been disappearing because he's been her love slave. That's all we need. . . .

"Looking for your friend Harris, Summers?"

Buffy whirled around to see Snyder. As usual, they stood eye to eye—it always gave Buffy sadistic pleasure to note that she was the same height as their principal—and he had a vicious smile on his face. *Which, come to think of it, is the only smile I've ever seen him use, outside of the night with the band candy, anyhow.*

"No, I, uh—" She hesitated, not wanting to get Xander in trouble.

"I excused him from the assembly. Not something I'd normally do for a student of Harris's meager accomplishments, but he'd already signed up for a ring. That shows a spirit I hadn't credited him with having, so I let him go. I occasionally provide these magnanimous gestures to—"

"Fool people into thinking you have a heart?" Buffy asked with a sweet smile.

Reverting to his more typical scowl, Snyder then said, "I can't help but notice, Summers, that you haven't signed up for a ring. No time like the present."

Her own smile also falling, Buffy stared at the floor, hoping the linoleum would provide solace. It didn't. "I can't. I wanted to—really, I did—but we can't afford it."

Snyder shook his head. "Always some excuse. 'I can't afford it, Principal Snyder,' 'Rings make my finger turn green, Principal Snyder,' 'The IRS just did an audit, Principal Snyder.' Kids..." He wagged a finger at Buffy; she somehow resisted the urge to bite it. "Mark my words, Summers, you're walking on thin ice. There are still four months left in the school year, and that's plenty of time for you to revert to form and give me just the excuse I need to expel you a second time." The smile came back, and Snyder straightened up. "I've never expelled anyone twice before. The very thought has me all a-quiver."

"I'm thrilled for you," Buffy deadpanned, trying to suppress her nausea.

"Try to stay out of trouble, Summers. Or better yet, don't."

With that, the principal wandered off to find someone else to annoy.

Willow and Oz appeared at Buffy's side. Her

instinct was to complain that they hadn't come to her rescue sooner, but that wasn't fair. Snyder would've just trapped them in his web of malice like some kind of bald, big-eared spider.

"Everything okay?" Willow sounded concerned.

Buffy tried to shrug it off. "Just Snyder being Snyder. Like he said, there's only four months left, and then we'll never have to deal with him again." She grinned. "The very thought has me all a-quiver. C'mon, let's go check out our praying mantis."

As soon as they climbed out of Oz's van, which he'd parked in the municipal lot across the street from the sort-of-nonexistent Dryanushkina house, Willow tensed right up.

"Will?" Buffy asked.

Oz put a hand on her shoulder. "You all right?"

Willow blinked twice, looked at Oz as if she'd never seen him before in her life, then shook her head. "I'm fine. I just—that was weird."

Unable to stifle a small smile, Buffy asked, "We talkin' 'I'm confused' weird or 'this is gonna strangle us in our sleep' weird?"

"I'm not sure." Willow hesitated. "You know how I have a protection spell on me, right?"

Buffy didn't know, actually, but Oz nodded quickly. "Right, you said it's a basic precaution."

Willow nodded right back. "As soon as we came out of the van, the spell went all oogly on me." She pointed across the street. "It's coming from there. Buffy, whatever magic's happening there, it's *way* beyond me." Then she looked down. "Well, to be fair, David Copperfield's way beyond me, but you know what I mean."

Reaching into her duffel bag, Buffy said, "Worry not, Will. Have machete, will travel." She removed the weapon and held it aloft. "Let's go."

They crossed the street and walked past the mailbox, which was still labeled Y. DRYANUSHKINA, just like it had been last night.

Willow suddenly stopped walking. "Oh, no. No-no-no-no-no. Buffy, this is wrong—it's all completely wrong."

"Not bad," said a new voice. "Most mages who'd studied as little as you would only see a house."

Buffy whirled around to see a little woman with short dark hair flecked with gray, a round face, small eyes, and a button nose standing in the doorway of the house, smiling sweetly. She wore an ankle-length short-sleeved gray dress that was only one step above wearing a burlap sack. *Pretty much what you'd expect from a sub.* She spoke with an obvious Russian accent, but it wasn't so thick that she couldn't be understood.

"You must be Yulia Dryanushkina," Buffy said, pronouncing it, as she had all along, "Dry-ah-nush-*kee*-nuh."

The woman laughed—actually, she tittered, which Buffy found kind of disturbing. "It's pronounced 'Dry-ah-*noosh*-kin-ah.'"

"Gesundheit. Would you mind telling me why vampires and witches go wiggy whenever they come near your place?"

"You may put the weapon down, Buffy Summers—or do you prefer 'Slayer'? Either way, I can assure you, the knife will do you little good."

"How do you know my name?"

"And what you are?" Yulia smiled broadly. "I know many things, Slayer, including that your friend Willow Rosenberg there has been studying the ways of magic for barely a year, and that your other friend Daniel Osborne has been a werewolf for approximately as long. I also know that your Watcher is named Rupert Giles and that he works in the Sunnydale High School Library. I'm surprised that you didn't bring your friend Alexander Harris."

Buffy had not lowered her weapon, nor did she have any intention of doing so, muttering, "I'll take 'Slayers and Friends' for one thousand, Alex."

"Come into my house, why don't you?"

Willow leaned forward. "Buffy, no. There's something—"

"Please do not whisper," Yulia said. "It's rude."

Holding the machete up higher, Buffy said, "Oh, I'm gonna get a *lot* ruder if you don't start answering my questions."

"Thus far, you've only asked one that I have not answered."

"Two, actually," Buffy said. "'I know many things' doesn't really cut it as an answer. And if you don't start—"

Yulia raised her arms and started whispering something. As soon as she did, every hair on Buffy's body, from the back of her neck to the phantom hair from when she shaved her legs that morning, began to stand on end.

The house started to get all fuzzy, and Buffy felt a chill despite the SoCal sunlight. Beneath her feet, the grass on which Buffy stood shimmered. Through her boots, she could actually feel the ground change from the soft lawn to the compact dirt that she had seen on Willow's laptop screen.

But it was what had happened to the house that freaked Buffy out. No longer was it a typical Sunnydale split-level, but a giant house that looked like it had come, fittingly, right out of an old fairy tale: big, thatched roof, walls made of what looked like hardened mud, square windows, and a big wooden door, which was open.

That wasn't even the weirdest part.

The house didn't touch the ground. Instead, it was balanced on each of the four corners by what Buffy would swear were giant chicken legs.

Three steps extended down from the doorway. Yulia was standing on the middle step. To Buffy's surprise, she was still wearing the same gray dress.

Willow's eyes had gotten wide as saucers. "You're Baba Yaga, aren't you?"

Buffy shot Willow a glance. "Baba who?"

"Very good, young mage," Yulia said with a smile. "I have had many names over the last ten thousand years, but Baba Yaga is the most common."

Leaning over to Buffy, Willow said, "Remember how I said I'd read up on all those fairy tales? Well, there were a bunch with Baba Yaga, and most of them talked about her hut on chicken legs."

Oz, looking as close to nonplussed as he ever did—which mostly just meant his eyes got a tiny bit narrower—said, "So those are *actual* chicken legs."

"Indeed they are, young werewolf," Yulia—or, rather, Yaga—said. "Now, then, shall we retire indoors?"

Even though Yaga was found in various Russian fairy tales, the ones this house reminded Buffy most of were the ones with Hansel and Gretl. In particular, she was concerned about what had happened to those two when they went into some old lady's funny-looking home. Ovens and cannibalism had been involved, which were not on Buffy's agenda.

As if reading Buffy's mind, Yaga said, "Or perhaps we should adjourn to your library? You would be more at ease there, I'm sure. Besides, I'm sure Mr. Rupert Giles will wish to hear what I have to say. It's of great import to all of us."

"What is?"

"Why, the imminent resurrection of Koschei, of course. I see you have your own vehicle. Shall we?"

Willow frowned. "Don't you have your mortar?"

Again, Buffy shot Willow a look. "She uses explosives?"

Yaga tittered again. "Not that kind of mortar, Slayer. She means the type with a pestle. I have a large one that can fly. And while that served me well in the Russian forests of times past, it would be a bit conspicuous in southern California now—even in *this* metropolis."

"Fine." Buffy pointed in the direction of Oz's van with her machete. "After you."

Yaga stepped down toward the trio. As she did, the ground shimmered once again, and the hut reverted back to the illusory house of Yulia Dryanushkina, retired substitute teacher, which came to Buffy as something of a relief. That hut was just *wrong*.

Oz went ahead to unlock the van, Willow by his side. Buffy, however, wasn't letting Yaga out of her sight, and let the woman go ahead of her. Buffy brought up the rear, keeping the machete handy, even though it really wasn't the weapon of choice against an immortal Russian sorceress.

All in all, I'd have preferred another praying mantis. . . .

Chapter Four

"So you're Baba Yaga."

Giles said those words from his position standing at the main desk of the library. Buffy was still holding the machete—though it was now in her lap—as she sat at the bottom of the staircase that led up to the stacks. They hadn't planned it, but they had both moved instinctively to those spots when Yaga moved to the center of the library. Buffy wasn't sure what, exactly, she or Giles could do against someone who could disguise her chicken-legged hut and a vacant lot as a suburban paradise, but she felt better with herself and Giles in flanking positions. Willow and Oz were sitting at the table.

"Yes, Avatar of Eyghon, I am indeed Baba Yaga."

Giles immediately removed his glasses and started polishing them furiously. Buffy was tempted to heft the machete again. Giles's raising of the demon Eyghon when he was younger—and the demon's return a year ago—wasn't a particularly fond memory for any of them, least of all Giles himself. Buffy already had Yaga low on her list, but she was about to supplant Snyder for the bottom spot.

"You . . ." Giles hesitated, then composed himself. "According to what I've read, you can control dead things."

Rolling her eyes, Buffy said, "Great, another necrophiliac?"

Yaga flashed her broad smile again. "Necro-*mancer*, if you please, Slayer. And, yes, I can control dead things—and that includes vampires."

A voice came from the doorway. "So that's why they avoid you like the plague."

Buffy looked over to see Faith entering.

"Ah, the second Slayer," Yaga said.

Grinning, Faith said, "Already told her about me, B?"

"No," Buffy said tightly, "she already knew all about both of us."

Her grin falling, Faith walked over to the cage and leaned against it. Yaga, Buffy noted with satisfaction, was now surrounded on three sides.

Faith started picking at her cast. "So, you make vamps go all kooky, huh?"

"Yes. They tend to steer clear of me, because they can sense my power over them. In general, vampires and I have a simple arrangement: They stay away from me, and I do not force them to sunbathe."

Giles, however, wasn't finished. "You are also invariably described as an older woman, yet you look no older than I."

"That kinda makes her older," Buffy said. To her credit, she looked apologetic as soon as the words left her mouth.

For his part, Giles started polishing his glasses again, as he clarified. "An *elderly* woman. 'Bony-legged' was a particularly common description, and you're often called 'Grandmother.'"

Yaga folded her arms over her chest. "You are well-read. However, I am immortal and may alter my visage as I wish. Appearing as an old woman served my purposes once. Appearing as I do serves my purposes now."

Willow shook her head. "I don't understand. If you're an immortal Russian sorceress, why are you in Sunnydale? Don't you make people do menial tasks in return for some kind of magical favor or something?"

"You are also well-read," Yaga said. "Those stories are a bit—exaggerated, shall we say. In any event, to answer your question, I left Russia in 1917. Communism and magic, you see, do not mix well."

"I imagine not," Giles said, having finally finished polishing his glasses. "How long have you been here?"

"For a while. I was here before you or your Slayer were, certainly."

Hefting her machete, Buffy got up from the staircase. "We have names, lady. I suggest you start using them, or I start using this."

Now Yaga put her hands on her hips. "Indeed?

Very well, Ms. Summers. Have I answered Mr. Giles's question?"

"Yes," Giles said, replacing his spectacles, "though it prompts another: Why have you chosen to reveal yourself now? You could have hidden from Buffy and the others in any number of ways, yet you chose to go public, as it were. Why?"

"I should think that would be obvious, Mr. Giles. The reason is Koschei. The time is ripe for his resurrection, and I would dislike it very much if that came to pass."

"How come?" Willow asked.

Yaga turned to Willow and smiled again. "Because I'm the one who killed him."

Willow's eyes widened, and in a very small voice she said, "Oh."

"This metropolis is a hive of magical activity, which I have monitored very closely. I know of you, Ms. Rosenberg, your friends Mr. Czajak and Ms. Madison—now, sadly, transmogrified into vermin—I know of your mentor, the late Ms. Calendar, I know of the equally late Master and his attempts at rising, and I know of Mr. Giles's former friend Mr. Rayne and any number of other things I could mention, but I believe, from the look on Ms. Summers's face, I should cease there."

Buffy had actually moved closer to Yaga, machete at the ready. "I've had it with your little trivia recitations, Ms. Dryanushkina." She deliberately mispronounced the necromancer's name.

If she was put off by it, Yaga showed no outward

sign. "My apologies, Ms. Summers. I was merely try-ing to prove a point."

"That being?"

"That I am who I say I am, and that I am not to be trifled with."

Buffy smiled. "If you know as much as you say you do, then you should know that I trifle with pretty much whoever I want. Now, you said you know Koschei's supposed to be resurrected. Can you stop it?"

Yaga stared at Buffy for several seconds. Buffy stared right back.

Finally, Yaga looked away and started pacing, which Buffy considered a moral victory.

"Possibly. It won't be easy. This metropolis is rather short on necromancers."

"Well, there's you," Faith said snidely.

"I was the one who killed Koschei," Yaga said with equal snideness. "I'm hardly likely to resurrect him a thousand years later."

"Says you."

Oz suddenly spoke up. "I'm a little confused about something. What's the big deal if this Koschei guy gets resurrected?"

Giles walked a few steps toward where Oz sat. "The material Valery sent me paints a rather disturbing picture of Koschei's evil tendencies."

"Yeah, but those are just stories, right?" Oz said. "Do we have any proof?"

Yaga turned her back on Faith, ignored Oz, and looked directly at Buffy and Giles. "I realize that you may not trust me, but you can trust this: The *Vozrozhdeniye* requires the life essence of many living souls to be sacrificed in order for the resurrection to occur. Many will die so Koschei can live. If you think that is not worth your time—"

"We do," Buffy said emphatically. Oz had raised a good point, though, and Buffy still didn't trust this woman as far as she could throw the lady's hut. "Giles, is that true?"

"Hm? Oh, yes, the *Vozrozhdeniye* does require death on a rather appalling scale."

"Fine." Buffy now looked back at Yaga. "How do we stop him?"

Yaga said, "There is a counterspell that will halt the *Vozrozhdeniye*. However, in order to cast it I will need an apprentice. I have not had one for several years. The last one blew up a perfectly good parking garage." She turned to look at the table. "I believe Ms. Rosenberg can serve that role."

Willow straightened. "What? No! I can't! I mean—I don't want to be a necromancer. It's icky! No offense . . ."

Yaga shrugged. "Very well. I shall simply instruct all the vampires in this town—including your precious Angel—to attack your homes tonight. And perhaps I'll make Angel take a walk on the beach tomorrow at dawn."

That was the straw that broke Buffy's back. She raised the machete and moved toward Yaga, but found she couldn't lower her arms to strike the sorceress.

"O-o-okay."

Faith then leapt at Yaga, but fell short of the mark, and couldn't strike her either.

"What the hell *is* this, B?"

Yaga tittered, a sound Buffy was truly learning to despise. "I wove a protection spell against the Slayer two centuries ago. It has proven useful on more than one occasion. No Slayer may bring harm to my person. And there is little point in your trying. Within a week the conditions under which Koschei can be revived will have passed. Once that has happened, I promise, Slayers, that you will never see me again."

Buffy glanced at Faith, who looked as angry as Buffy had ever seen her, for which Buffy could hardly blame her. Finally, she lowered the machete to her side. "Fine. What's the next step?"

"Ms. Rosenberg and I return to my home to gather the necessary spell components. Then—"

"No," Buffy said.

"Excuse me?"

"Willow's not going anywhere with you. If you need to go home and stock up, that's fine, but you're not taking her with you. I don't care what kind of protection against Slayers you've got, there's no *way* you're going to be alone with my friend. Understood?"

That prompted another smile. "Whatever you say, Ms. Summers."

With that, Yaga turned on her heel and departed.

Oz asked, "How's she gonna get back? She came in my van."

"That's her problem," Buffy said, walking over to

the cage. "Sorry, Faith—I didn't know we couldn't attack her."

"Not a problem, B," Faith said, looking at the door. "But that lady and me are gonna have words before this is all over."

"Get in line," Buffy said quietly, then opened the cage to replace the machete.

"Behind me as well," Giles said. "Still, while I agree that she is irritating, we will need her if Koschei is resurrected. Valery's papers have made it abundantly clear that our own magical abilities will not be sufficient to meet the task. Besides, Valery also discusses Baba Yaga, and describes her as both reclusive and annoying, but not dangerous. The fact that we've heard neither hide nor hair of her in three years supports that."

"I guess." Buffy only agreed with the greatest reluctance.

Willow raised her hand. "Giles? I *really* don't want to be a necromancer."

"I'm relieved to hear it," Giles said dryly. "Don't worry, Willow, we'll make sure Yaga doesn't do any lasting harm to your magical studies. Still, your assistance will be of use to her—and to us, as well. I'd feel more secure if one of us was keeping an eye on her."

"Preferably someone who can actually hit her," Buffy muttered.

"Hitting?" Willow looked nervous. "I'm no good with the hitting."

"I was kidding, Will." Buffy actually wasn't, but Willow looked relieved, which was what Buffy was going for.

"Still," Giles said, "best if we do more research of our own—about Koschei and the *Vozrozhdeniye*."

"You kids have fun," Faith said. "Me, I need to hit something."

"Or a lot of somethings," Buffy said. "We're gonna patrol. I'll check in later, see what you found."

Giles nodded. "Good luck."

"You, too. I'd rather we didn't have to rely on chicken-leg lady for the 411 on this Koschei guy."

Chapter Five

After the previous night, Buffy and Faith had had their fill of cemeteries, and besides, Faith had heard one of her neighbors at the flophouse talking about some weird guys hanging out under one of the freeway overpasses. Apparently, the homeless population had been disappearing one by one.

"If we're lucky," Faith had said when she told Buffy about it, "we'll get a whole nest of vamps to dust."

"Works for me" had been Buffy's response.

Rovello Drive—the street Buffy lived on—stretched all the way across Sunnydale. Down at Buffy's end, it was nice and residential. As one traveled farther west, though, it boasted vacant lot after vacant lot, and then curved under the 418, a state freeway that served as an artery to the 5, the interstate highway that ran all the way up the West Coast.

The pillars that supported the 418 were pock-marked and covered in graffiti. Above them, cars zoomed by at great speeds, loud enough that anybody below screaming in pain from, say, having their blood drained by a vampire, wouldn't be heard.

Rovello's sidewalk disappeared as soon as it went under the 418, replaced by uneven rocks and dirt that extended under the overpass. There weren't any street lights out here, either, so it was progressively darker the farther under the freeway one ventured.

Under other circumstances Buffy would have been a bit more cautious, but she'd spent the afternoon being pissed off by Snyder and the evening being pissed off by Baba Yaga, and she was in the mood to commit some serious violence.

"Hey, B! Over here."

Faith had gone a few steps ahead. Buffy looked down Rovello to see that she had stopped and was standing over something.

Buffy jogged over to see the something was a body. She could tell it was a man by the rat's nest of a beard that combined with his wild hair to obscure everything except his big nose and his eyes. His clothes hadn't been laundered since Angel was in diapers, and his coat had so many holes, Buffy could see more of the lining than the coat itself. He had two puncture wounds in his neck, which Buffy could easily detect because the vampire who killed him had brushed aside that part of the beard.

"We got us a feeding spot," Faith said.

Buffy nodded.

"Can't believe these guys'd go for this, though. I mean, this guy's wicked smelly."

"There are two Slayers in town. That makes it twice as hard to find a good meal." Buffy took out her stake. "And we're about to make it harder."

"Oh, I doubt that."

Buffy looked up to see half a dozen vampires moving in from all directions. Most of them were almost as badly dressed as the victim at Faith's feet, though none of them were having the same sort of bad-hair day. She guessed that they were dressed this way to blend in, making it easier to take their homeless prey.

The one who'd spoken had short blond hair and a brown goatee. "It's about time you two showed up." He looked at Faith. "I was gonna leave a Post-It on your door next."

"This was a setup?" Buffy asked.

"Obviously. We're tired of you two forcing us down here to eat garbage. We want our town back. We figure, with you two gone, the next Slayer'll be somewhere else. Outer Mongolia, maybe. But not here, which is all we give a damn about."

Nodding, Buffy said, "Good plan."

"Thanks, I was kinda proud of it, actually."

"You should be. Shows good foresight. I'm impressed."

The blond vampire smiled. "Thanks! That's good of you to say."

"There's just one itty-bitty problem."

"What, that we haven't actually killed you yet? I

realize that, but there are six of us and two of you. In case you flunked math at that pathetic school of yours, that's three-to-one odds. Know what that's called?"

Faith grinned. "A mismatch." Then she threw a rock that Buffy hadn't noticed her pick up right at the blond guy's head.

The vampires were sufficiently taken aback by that move, and they were rendered sitting ducks for Buffy and Faith each to attack with a jumping side kick.

His hand pressed to the bleeding gash on his head, the blond said, "Don't just stand there, you jackasses, *kill them*!"

One of them leapt at Buffy, but she dodged effortlessly out of the way. The vampire she had kicked leapt to her feet and tried a spin kick, but Buffy kicked right back, knocking her down again, then elbowed the first one in the face, extended her arm, and drove down her stake.

Unfortunately, she missed the heart, impaling the vampire only in the shoulder. *Dammit.*

Grabbing the stake out of Buffy's hand, the vampire tossed it under the overpass. Buffy quickly lost it amidst the rocks and other bits of garbage strewn about.

The vampire grinned, fangs bared.

Another vampire, a red-haired woman, got Buffy in a bear hug from behind. The man came closer, joined by the blond ringleader. Buffy could see that Faith was being hemmed in by the other three.

"It's a mismatch all right," the blond guy said. "You'll be dead in a min—"

The redhead still had Buffy in the bear hug, so she just used her as a lever as she jumped up and kicked out with both feet before the blond guy could finish his sentence. Her boots nailed both vampires' jaws, and down they went. Buffy then stepped on each of the redhead's feet with her one-inch boot heels in succession, bent forward, and straightened up really fast. The back of her skull smashed into the bridge of the redhead's nose, dazing her enough to loosen her grip. Buffy grabbed the redhead's arm and whirled around, throwing the vampire into the blond guy, who was just getting to his feet. They collapsed in a giant heap.

Buffy ran toward the overpass, near where her stake had been thrown.

"You stupid bitch, you're not gonna find your stake there!" the blond yelled.

Ignoring him, Buffy ran deeper into the dark overpass, hoping that she'd seen what she thought she'd seen. When she found the object she was seeking, she turned around and saw the blond guy and the one who'd taken her stake running toward her. The redhead was holding back.

Two will do, she thought. As soon as they got close, she bent over, picked up the busted two-by-four, shoved it forward into the blond guy's chest, then yanked it back.

The other vampire stood in shock as he saw his ringleader turned to dust before his eyes. "That wasn't part of the plan."

"It was part of mine." Buffy smiled sweetly, then kicked him in the face hard enough to send him sprawling. He managed to crabwalk out of the way of her second lunge with the two-by-four. That was when the redhead finally rejoined the fight.

The two vamps danced around Buffy, keeping their distance, not letting her get close with the makeshift stake—but also not getting close enough to hurt her.

Then Buffy heard a cry of pain, and looked away for a second to see that Faith had fallen to the pavement and was now being kicked repeatedly in the ribs by the other three vampires. No, make that two vampires—*Faith must have staked one. Good for her.*

"Faith!" Buffy cried out, trying to sound panicky.

Her two opponents figured Buffy was distracted by her fellow Slayer in distress, and lunged. Buffy had been counting on that. With a grunt she slammed her two-by-four into one of them.

Even as the guy turned into dust, though, along with the two-by-four, the redhead body-slammed Buffy, and they collapsed onto the rocks and dirt.

And broken glass, Buffy thought with annoyance as the remnants of a beer bottle sliced into her cheek. She reached across her body, grabbed the busted glass, and swung at the redhead with it, just as she was about to bite Buffy's neck.

They both got to their feet and faced each other. The redhead snarled. Buffy brandished the broken bottle.

Suddenly, an unfamiliar voice said, "I would suggest leaving those girls alone, okay?"

Both Buffy and her foe turned to see where the voice was coming from.

It was a man, not very tall, but with muscles to die for, which Buffy could see clearly, as he was wearing a sleeveless shirt and tight jeans. He had short hair, and even in this poor light Buffy noticed that he had the most *amazing* blue eyes. Good-looking buff guys weren't exactly uncommon in Southern California, but what made this guy stand out was that he carried a very big sword.

He also spoke with a Russian accent. *What, is there a convention in town?*

With one fluid motion he jumped forward and swung his sword around, cleanly beheading one of the vampires kicking Faith; the vampire disintegrated a moment later. Faith took advantage of this development and kicked her final attacker in the back of the knee. He fell forward, right onto Faith's stake.

Looking at the redhead, Buffy said, "Three-to-one odds. Know what that's called?"

The vampire, whose back was to the overpass, turned and ran into the darkness.

Buffy hesitated. She did *not* want to follow her—vampires had much better night vision than humans, and Buffy would be blind in there.

However, the buff Russian guy didn't pause for a second. "You do not get away that easily, okay?"

A moment later, he, too, disappeared beneath the overpass.

Buffy jogged over to Faith, who was clambering to her feet, using her left arm for support. "You okay?"

Clutching her abdomen with her left arm, Faith said, "My ribs're pissed at me, but I'll live." She looked into the darkness of the overpass. "Who was that masked man?"

"I don't know, but did you catch the accent?"

Faith nodded. "It's like I'm back in Brookline." Buffy assumed that to be a Boston neighborhood that had a high Russian population. "This is gettin' seriously screwy, B."

A form started to become visible in the darkness. Buffy stiffened, her fists in front of her, ready for a fight. Next to her, Faith made an approximation of doing likewise, but she was obviously hobbled by new cracks in her not-quite-healed ribs.

Seconds later, Buffy lowered her fists. The form was male and carrying a sword. He was also smiling broadly. Buffy couldn't help but notice that his teeth were perfect. His skin was smooth and bronze and incredibly powerful, and— *Dammit, Summers, put your hormones on hold, will you?*

"Nice work there, Ivan," Faith said. Buffy noticed that her fellow Slayer's eyes were also on those sculpted muscles.

"Not quite," he said.

"Excuse me?" Buffy said, shoving her lust into the same dark corner she put distracting thoughts of Brad Pitt, George Clooney, and Angel when she needed to focus. "Oh, and by the way, who *are* you?"

"I am not Ivan," the man said with a smile. "That was the name of my dearest friend a long time ago. I am Bulat, and I have come to warn you."

Buffy remembered that "Bulat the Brave" was one of the names Willow had thrown out along with those of Baba Yaga and Koschei. *There really is a convention in town.* "We know, someone's about to resurrect Koschei the Deathless. That's old news."

"I am aware that you are aware of Koschei's imminent return to this plane of existence. That is not what I wish to warn you about. Or, rather, who."

"What who?" Buffy asked.

"You must be wary of Baba Yaga. She is not to be trusted, and everything she has told you is a lie."

Buffy looked at Faith. Faith shrugged and said, "Don't look at me, B. I'm just the girl that hits things."

"Yeah." Buffy let out a long sigh. "How'd you like to join us on a trip to the Sunnydale High School Library, Bulat?"

"What is there?" Bulat asked.

Relieved that there was a Russian fairy-tale protagonist in town who *didn't* know her entire life story, Buffy said, "My Watcher, for one thing. C'mon."

"Okay." Bulat walked over to the street and picked something up off the ground. It was, Buffy realized, a scabbard attached to a string. Bulat tied the string around his waist, then put the sword in the scabbard. Buffy took that moment to admire his muscles some more. "It gets in the way when fighting—bounces around too much, okay?"

Faith put on her most feral grin. "It's okay by me, stud."

Buffy rolled her eyes. *Not that I'm one to judge, since I've been checking him out since he got here.* "Let's go."

As they walked back up Rovello Drive Buffy

thought, *Why couldn't it just have been a praying mantis? I'd have hacked it to pieces and skipped Ring Day in peace.*

"You cannot trust Baba Yaga," the man who claimed to be Bulat the Brave said as he sat comfortably at the table, flanked on either side by Buffy and Faith. Giles couldn't help but notice that both girls were admiring Bulat's well-muscled form, which the warrior had put on display.

While Giles had his doubts that this was necessarily the same Bulat the Brave spoken of in Russian legend (not to mention Valery's notes), he was comfortable with the "warrior" label. First of all, Buffy and Faith had seen him behead vampires with his sword—and, their potential lust notwithstanding, neither was prone to exaggeration in that particular regard—which was a difficult feat to accomplish, as it required a precision and strength that only came from years of swordplay. Bulat also walked with the gait of a man who was used to having a scabbard at his side—something else that only came with many years of having one there.

"And why should we trust *you*, exactly?" Giles asked.

Bulat blinked his deep blue eyes in surprise. "I aided your Slayers and saved their lives, okay?"

"Hey, don't push it, gorgeous." Faith pointed an accusatory finger at the Russian. "There were only six of them, and me an' B had everything in hand."

"Was that before or after the two vampires had you

down and were kicking you repeatedly in the ribs?"
Bulat asked tartly.

"I was just regrouping," Faith said with a smile.
"But, hey, you don't buy it, why don't we throw down
right here?" She got up, tossing her chair aside.

As Bulat started to rise in response, Giles held up a
hand. "Enough! Faith, sit down, please. I do not
believe that the combat prowess of anyone in this room
is in question."

Bulat gave Giles an incredulous look, and then
laughed. "If you say so."

Resisting the urge to make a boast of his own—it
would only sound ridiculous, and besides, he'd just
admonished Faith for the same thing—Giles simply
continued: "What concerns me is whether or not
there's any truth to your word."

"I have no reason to lie."

"Not that we are aware of."

Buffy finally spoke up. "Look, Giles, why don't
we just let him say his peace? Obviously, he knows
something. Let's find out what it is."

Giles thought that her interest was as much in
keeping the "hunky stud" around as anything, then he
dismissed the notion as unfair, mainly because Buffy
wasn't *that* shallow, but also because she was correct.

"Very well," Giles said. "Why can Baba Yaga not
be trusted?"

"She lies. She misleads. She tricks. She is a sorceress, okay? People who wield magic cannot be trusted."

"Really?" Giles said dryly. He also noticed Buffy
tensing, no doubt on Willow's behalf. Giles was grate-

ful that she had gone home shortly before Buffy and Faith's arrival with this latest character.

Bulat shifted in his seat. It looked as if he was starting to understand how skeptical his audience was, which was apparently not what he had been expecting. "I do not understand. I rescued you. I fought by your side."

Giles, though, was starting to comprehend the situation. "I can see why you would feel this way."

Shooting Giles a confused look, Buffy asked, "Could you maybe provide closed captioning for the macho logic-impaired?"

"Yeah," Faith said. "We scrap, that means you got my gratitude, but that's it."

"This gentleman comes from a warrior ethic." Giles started pacing as he spoke. "Where he comes from, fighting side by side is an unbreakable bond, one that creates instant camaraderie." He smirked slightly. "It was a simpler time."

"I was gonna go for a stupider time, but whatever." Buffy turned to Bulat. "Either way, you're gonna have to do more than decapitate a couple vamps before we bond."

"Okay." Bulat let out a long breath. "I will tell you story. When I am finished, you decide if Baba Yaga is to be trusted, okay?"

"Fire away," Buffy said, leaning back in her chair.

Bulat nodded. "Okay. I will tell the story the way my good friend Prince Ivan always told it over the years. It began when I made the mistake of not repaying a debt to a merchant who was friends with Koschei the Deathless."

Chapter Six

Russia, once upon a time . . .

•

Prince Ivan had spent the last several weeks wandering through the land that would one day become his kingdom. He had told his father, the king, that he was going in search of a bride, but that was not the true reason. While his nursemaid had sung a lullaby to him when he was a baby about how he would find the love of his life "beyond thrice nine lands in the thrice tenth kingdom," Ivan had never given those stories much credit. The nursemaid had even provided a name—Vasilisa Kirbitievna—but there were no Kirbitievnas or Kirbitievovs of noble blood anywhere nearby.

Besides, Ivan didn't want a wife. There'd be time enough for that when he was king and he was obligated to provide an heir. At that point he would be happy with whichever noblewoman his advisors suggested, as long as she would bear him a strong son to take over the kingdom when Ivan died. For now, though, he was content to live the happy life of a confirmed bachelor. After all, he was a prince, and what good was being a prince if he could not do what he wished?

He arrived at a village, and left his squire to tend to the horses while he walked through town. Ivan hadn't wanted to make a fuss about his tour, so he was not dressed in princely garb and hadn't brought any of his bodyguards. He had only brought the squire to take care of the horses. The king had agreed to this solely because Ivan had convinced him that he needed to find his bride without the distractions of royalty.

In truth, Ivan found his bodyguards tiresome. He wanted to roam unfettered throughout the land, to *see* his people, not as a prince saw them, but as they saw one another.

It was apparently market day in this village, as most of the population seemed to be gathered in a large square that was packed with carts and stands selling all manner of merchandise. Ivan noted a fruit cart, at which point his stomach started to rumble. Realizing that he hadn't eaten all day, he looked through the strawberries, thinking it might be good to acquire some for a snack.

He argued with the owner of the fruit cart over the price for the strawberries. The prince could, of course, afford the first price the vendor quoted, and it wasn't as if Ivan had any notion of what a fair price would actually be, but he wanted to act like a normal person, so he haggled.

Then he heard a scream.

"What is that?" Ivan asked, looking behind him.

"It is nothing," the vendor said. "Fifteen rubles."

"Ten, and not a ruble more," Ivan said. Another scream. "Screaming like that cannot be 'nothing.'"

"You are taking the food from my family's table, but I will generously lower my offer to fourteen rubles. And it is simply someone being flogged in the square. He has obviously broken a law and is being punished. That is the way of things."

Ivan and the vendor finally settled on eleven rubles, the vendor swearing that he would be forced out of business by his embarrassing generosity.

The prince then followed the sound of the screaming to see a man being flogged with a leather strap. The man doing the flogging was dressed in armor that indicated a position of military authority. The man being flogged was large and bronzed, indicating a life spent out of doors, and his well-toned muscles bespoke a life spent doing hard work. He was stripped to the waist, but his leather leggings were for protection, and the belt on those leggings had a place for a scabbard. In all likelihood the man was a swordsman, possibly a mercenary.

What Ivan noted in particular about the man being flogged were his blue eyes, which he opened between strokes of the lash, and which were as deep as the sea.

Another man wearing the same armor as the one doing the flogging stood watching. Ivan assumed him to be a supervisor of some sort and approached him.

"Who is this man and what has he done to deserve this treatment?"

"He borrowed ten thousand rubles from a merchant and did not pay him back at the agreed time."

"What if I agree to pay the ten thousand rubles?"

"That would be unwise," the man said. "Whoever redeems this man will suffer to have his wife taken from him by Koschei the Deathless."

At that, Ivan threw his head back and laughed. "I shall redeem this man."

The supervisor looked upon Ivan with surprise. "Are you a madman, that you do not fear the consequences?"

"I am no madman, sir, but I *am* a bachelor. I have no wife for Koschei the Deathless to take." He reached into the money pouch from which he had taken the eleven rubles for the strawberries. "I have 689 rubles in this pouch. When my squire returns from the stables, I shall provide the remaining 9,311."

"Very well, then," the supervisor said. He gestured to the man wielding the strap, who ceased his flogging.

It took the man being flogged several seconds to realize that his punishment had ceased. He slowly got to his feet.

Ivan approached him. "You are free. I have redeemed you. Your debt is paid."

The man's eyes grew wide with fear. "I thank you, but do you know what you have done? Your wife will be taken by Koschei the Deathless!"

"I have no wife, and therefore have nothing to fear from the mighty sorcerer."

"I am called Bulat the Brave," the man told Ivan.

"My name is Ivan. Come, let us find you some suitable clothing, and you may join me."

Ivan treated Bulat to a meal at the inn attached to the stable where Ivan's squire had put the horses. They planned to stay the night and then proceed on their respective quests the next day. Bulat no longer had any business in this village, and he was on his way to meet a woman. Ivan asked who this woman was.

"Her name is Vasilisa Kirbitievna."

The prince almost choked on his food. That was the same name provided by his nursemaid when he was a boy.

Deciding to trust Bulat, Prince Ivan told him the truth, both about who he was and the reason for his travels.

"So you do not seek a bride?" Bulat asked.

"No, I do not. Brides are for kings, and I am a prince. But it is very strange that I would be told that I would someday marry a woman with the same name as the woman you are pursuing."

"It is strange," Bulat said. "In truth, Vasilisa is a woman beyond my station. I am a simple sword-for-hire, where she is the child of a minor nobleman in the kingdom on the other side of the mountain."

Again Ivan almost choked. The kingdom to which Bulat referred was the "thrice tenth kingdom" his nursemaid had sung to him about. He told this to Bulat.

"Truly it was meant for us to find each other, your highness," Bulat said with a big grin. "I was hoping to see Vasilisa one last time, for I know that she can never be mine. But if I bring you to her, then you shall have your princess, who shall one day be queen."

"But would that not make you sad, Bulat, to see the woman you love married to another?"

"All that matters is that she be happy, your highness. And what woman would not be happy as queen?"

And so Ivan and Bulat agreed to travel to the kingdom over the mountain to find Vasilisa Kirbitievna.

When they arrived, Bulat the Brave called upon Vasilisa, but he did not identify himself by name, instead saying that he had come on behalf of Prince Ivan. Bulat said that Vasilisa would probably not agree to see him publicly—all their liaisons had been in secret—but if he represented himself as being sent by the prince, he would be allowed in the front door.

Bulat and Ivan were brought into the moderate-size house where Vasilisa lived with her father. Her mother had died in childbirth and her father had never remarried. She was pretty, and Ivan's first thought upon seeing her stout form was that she would bear good sons, which was all one truly wanted from a queen.

She was pleasant and polite, and asked Prince Ivan many questions about his home, yet Ivan noticed that, all the time, she looked at Bulat.

At once, Ivan made his decision. He would bring Vasilisa back home with him to be his bride. Bulat would also return as his new bodyguard. This would allow Bulat and Vasilisa to see each other, as they clearly desired, and Ivan would have not just a future queen, but the very one that had been prophesied for him. It was a perfect plan, and one that could not possibly go wrong.

It took little work to secure Vasilisa's father's blessing, and before long they all proceeded out of the kingdom back over the mountains, and to Ivan's home. The squire rode ahead to announce their arrival, and a huge celebration was quickly organized by the king to welcome the prince home.

Over the next several years, Bulat and Ivan became constant companions. Bulat protected Ivan from harm, and Vasilisa as well when they traveled together. Vasilisa settled into her role as the prince's betrothed. At first Ivan preferred to put off the wedding until absolutely necessary, but when the king's health began to worsen, his advisors convinced Ivan that it was time to reassure the people that the royal line would continue.

It was a grand ceremony, one attended by the entire town, and many of those from other towns in the kingdom. Vasilisa's father traveled over the mountain to be there as well. There was much food and mead and beer, and the celebration went on for several days.

On the morning after the last of the marital celebrations had ended, Prince Ivan awoke to find that Princess Vasilisa was gone.

They searched the entire city, but of Vasilisa there was no sign. Bulat the Brave was beside himself, for he realized that it was his fault. "You were warned," Bulat said to Ivan, "that if you redeemed me, your wife would be carried off by Koschei the Deathless."

"But, Bulat," Ivan said, "that was years ago! And I had no wife at the time I redeemed you!"

"Koschei the Deathless is not one to be trifled with. He has hidden his death from the reaper, and so lives forever. One who lives forever has a long memory. I should never have permitted this. I am sorry, my friend, I have failed you."

Ivan tried to reassure Bulat. "You have done no such thing, my friend. Now do not worry—we command the greatest army in all of Russia. We will find Koschei the Deathless, and we will take our future queen back from him."

"No! Your highness, you must not do this! Koschei the Deathless is one of the greatest sorcerers who has ever lived! If you send your army after him, you will lose your army forever, and then your kingdom will be lost to its neighbors. No, I must go alone."

"That is madness, my friend," Ivan said. "One man cannot stop Koschei the Deathless if an army cannot."

"An army cannot stop him, and neither can one man. But one man can perhaps trick him."

With those words, Bulat the Brave struck out on his own.

Bulat's first destination was the forest, and a particular house that he knew was hidden within the trees.

It took him three days of walking, and three nights as well, but eventually he found the house he was looking for. It was surrounded by a fence, a skull adorning

the top of every post but one. The house itself stood
proudly, each of its corners balanced on a large
chicken leg.

This was the house of Baba Yaga, the one sorceress
who might be able to defeat Koschei.

Swallowing his fear that the empty post on the
fence would soon be adorned with his own skull, Bulat
approached the home of Baba Yaga. The door was
closed and he could not reach the knob. He knocked on
the bottom of the door and cried out, "Baba Yaga!
Answer the door! I have come to seek your advice!"

There was no answer, nor was there one the second
and third time he called out. Bulat decided that Baba
Yaga must not be home. So he waited in the forest for
her to return.

Night fell, and Baba Yaga did not come back. Bulat
continued to wait. He knew that the only way he would be
able to rescue Vasilisa Kirbitievna and stop Koschei the
Deathless would be to ask Baba Yaga the Bony-Legged
for help. The old woman knew the ways of magic. Bulat
had intended to come to Baba Yaga before, when he was
indebted to the merchant, but the town guard captured
him and flogged him before he could do so. Now, however, he was not a down-on-his-luck sword-for-hire, but
the bodyguard to Prince Ivan and Princess Vasilisa. He
could walk the land, and even walk the forests where
Baba Yaga hid from public view, without fear.

The next morning dawned, and Bulat was hungry.
He had only brought enough provisions for the journey
there and back. He had not expected to wait all the day
and all the night in the forest. The previous day, he had

seen many chickens wandering the yard in front of the house. So Bulat once again walked through the gate of skulls and, instead of going to the door, he went to the chicken coop, hoping to capture one and slaughter it for his breakfast.

Then Bulat heard a strange sound. He turned to see a giant mortar flying through the air, and in it stood an old woman with bony legs. She steered the mortar over the fence with a pestle and landed it in front of him.

"Are you Baba Yaga the Bony-Legged?" Bulat asked.

"I thought I smelled Russian breath in my yard. Who are you that invades my home unasked?"

"I am Bulat the Brave, and I seek advice. The woman I love has been taken by Koschei the Deathless because of my own foolishness. I must find her and rescue her and kill the sorcerer."

Baba Yaga laughed. "You are either very brave or very foolish, young Bulat. Why do you think you will succeed where others have failed?"

"I do not know, Grandmother, but I know that I must try. The woman I love is Princess Vasilisa."

"Interesting. Why would Koschei the Deathless take a princess?"

Bulat the Brave explained to Baba Yaga about the debt he owed the merchant, and the promise that any who redeemed him would have his wife taken by Koschei the Deathless.

"You said that Princess Vasilisa was the woman you loved. Yet she is married to another?"

"All I desire is Vasilisa's happiness. She would never marry a commoner such as I, but she will make a great queen one day. I must rescue her—for her, for myself, and for my friend Prince Ivan, who rescued me at such great risk. I will do whatever you ask in exchange for the knowledge of how to stop Koschei the Deathless."

Baba Yaga got out the mortar, gestured, and her mortar and pestle rose up and disappeared behind the house. "Very well, young Bulat. I will make you a bargain. I have a stable full of fine mares. You will spend the next three days caring for them. If one mare escapes the stable, then your head will go atop the final post on my fence. However, if you care for the mares and keep them all together, then I will reward you with the information you seek."

Bulat fell to his knees and thanked Baba Yaga for everything she did. Baba Yaga said she had done nothing yet, and that if Bulat wished to live to rescue his lady love, he should immediately go to the stables.

Now, Bulat was a mercenary by trade. While he knew how to ride a horse and how to feed one, he had never cared for an entire stable of them. Baba Yaga had thirteen mares, which did not make Bulat happy, as thirteen was an unlucky number.

Still, he did his best. He walked the horses around, made sure they ate and drank, fixed the shoe on one using a trick he'd learned from an old blacksmith friend, and chased down the ones that tried to run away. One mare had to be chased halfway across the forest, but Bulat found her and brought her back.

Luckily, Baba Yaga was away when that happened, so she would be none the wiser when she returned. In fact, Baba Yaga was often away from the house, but every time she returned, she came to the stables and counted the mares.

At the end of the third day, Baba Yaga came to him carrying a plate filled with roasted chicken and turnips. "You have done well, young Bulat," Baba Yaga said. "Come and eat this meal I have made for you, and I will tell you what you wish to know."

Bulat had been so afraid of having his head put on the last post on Baba Yaga's fence that he had forgotten his hunger. He had not eaten during the three days he cared for Baba Yaga's thirteen mares, so he greedily grabbed the plate and started to devour the chicken and turnips. Bulat had never particularly liked turnips, but today they were the most wonderful food in the entire world.

"I have gone to where Koschei the Deathless lives," Baba Yaga said, explaining where she'd been while she was away. "Before I could give you any advice, I had to find out if there was indeed a mission for you to undertake."

"I do not understand," Bulat said with a full mouth.

"Koschei the Deathless is an evil sorcerer who kidnaps people so he may kill them to extend his own life. In order to keep away his death, he must sacrifice others. However, Princess Vasilisa still lives. In fact, he has taken her as a lover."

Bulat threw his plate angrily upon the ground and rose to his feet.

Baba Yaga said, "Be calm, young Bulat, for the princess does not lie with Koschei willingly. She is his slave and must do as he bids, under penalty of death. She wishes to return to her life, and so she obeys him, hoping that Prince Ivan and his armies will rescue her."

That made Bulat even unhappier, for his lady love was counting, not on Bulat's love for her, but on Prince Ivan's armies, even though an army would be of no use against the mighty sorcerer.

"What must I do to bring her back?"

"Koschei goes out hunting in the mornings. He lets Princess Vasilisa ride by the pond while he is away. I will give you a charm that will transform you into a frog for one hour per day. You will use this charm to approach the princess at the pond and ask her where Koschei keeps his death."

"I do not understand," Bulat said. "Why can I not simply take her with me?"

"Because Koschei will know you have taken her and kill you both. The only way to rescue the princess is to kill Koschei, and the only way to kill Koschei is to give him back his death. He has found a way to hide it. Since he has taken the princess to his bed, he may confide in her. She must ask him where he keeps his death."

After a good night's sleep and a hearty breakfast, Baba Yaga sent Bulat the Brave on one of the thirteen mares—the difficult one that ran away, who was named Trudnaya—with the charm in hand that would turn him into a frog.

He rode for two days and nights before finally

arriving at the home of Koschei the Deathless. After making camp, he slept fitfully, awaiting the morning, when he would see his love again.

When morning came, he went to the pond on the outskirts of Koschei's lands, waiting for Vasilisa to begin her ride.

An hour passed, and another, and then finally he saw a white pony riding toward the pond with Vasilisa Kirbitievna astride it. Bulat gripped the charm and spoke the words Baba Yaga had told him. A moment later, he was a frog, and he leapt from lily pad to lily pad until he was near Vasilisa.

"Vasilisa! It is I, Bulat the Brave! I have come to rescue you!"

"You are but a frog—how can you rescue me?"

"This is a charm provided by Baba Yaga the Bony-legged. She has told me how to stop Koschei the Deathless."

Bulat the Brave explained the plan to Vasilisa, who said, "Very well. When Koschei returns from his hunt today, I will ask him where he keeps his death. Now I must ride on, for if I do not arrive back at the house at the appointed time, Koschei will be suspicious."

"Of course." Bulat hopped back to his camp and after an hour had passed, he became a man once again.

The next morning, he returned to the pond and again met Vasilisa as a frog. "Tell me, Vasilisa, where does Koschei keep his death?"

"I asked him last night," Vasilisa said, "and right away he told me that he kept it in the broom near the threshold."

Bulat the Brave had been a soldier for most of his life, and he knew that it could not be that easy. Vasilisa could not have been the first to ask such a question. "When you return to the house, I want you to decorate the broom with many ribbons and put it on the kitchen table. Tell him that his death should not just sit at the threshold thusly."

Vasilisa agreed, and she rode back to the house. Bulat the Brave hopped back to his camp, and after an hour had passed he became a man once again.

The next morning, he returned to the pond and again met Vasilisa as a frog. "Tell me, Vasilisa, what happened?"

"Koschei laughed at me. He said my hair is long, but my wit is short. He said his death was truly in the goat he gets his milk from."

Bulat the Brave told Vasilisa to do the same for the goat as she had for the broom. Vasilisa agreed, and she rode back to the house. Bulat the Brave hopped back to his camp, and after an hour had passed he became a man once again.

The next morning, he returned to the pond and again met Vasilisa as a frog. "Tell me, Vasilisa, what happened?"

"Koschei laughed at me again. He said that it was kind of me to wish to decorate his death so, but he did not keep it nearby. In the sea, he said, there is an island, and on that island stands an oak. A coffer is buried under the oak, and in that coffer is a nest of duck eggs. His death is in the largest of the eggs."

"Excellent," Bulat the Brave said. He told Vasilisa

to return to the house, and he would find Koschei's death and rescue her. Then he hopped back to his camp, and after an hour had passed he became a man once again and leapt onto Trudnaya.

It was a four-day journey to the sea, but Trudnaya was a fast mare, as Bulat had learned when he chased her down from Baba Yaga's stable. After only three days and two nights he came to the sea, where he hired a boat and stabled the mare. He rowed the boat out to the island with the oak, and then dug for the coffer. After an hour of digging he found the coffer and opened it to reveal a dozen eggs. Taking the largest and putting it in his pouch, he rowed back to the mainland and rode Trudnaya to Koschei's house. This time it only took two days and nights, for nothing now could keep Bulat from rescuing his love.

He arrived when Koschei was out on his hunt, so Bulat waited by the front door for his return. When he came back, Bulat said, "I carry a message from Prince Ivan for Koschei the Deathless. Are you him?"

"Yes, I am," Koschei the Deathless said, "but it matters little. There is nothing that Prince Ivan may say that will compel me to give back his wife. He knew the risks when he redeemed that fool, and nothing short of my death will stop me."

Bulat took the egg out of the pouch and said, "Then your death it shall be!" And he struck Koschei on the forehead with the egg, and Koschei the Deathless fell dead at his feet.

When Bulat the Brave returned with the princess,

they learned that the old king had died. Prince Ivan was now King Ivan, and Vasilisa was now queen. The celebrations went on for seven days and nights, and Ivan and Vasilisa continued to rule for many years, with Bulat the Brave beside them.

Chapter Seven

Sunnydale, California, February 1999

"**O**kay, I'm missing something."

Giles silently agreed with Buffy. From the sound of it, Baba Yaga had done precisely what was asked of her, and Bulat was able to rescue Vasilisa. His mistrust of Yaga seemed misplaced. Indeed, Giles himself had more reason to distrust Yaga, based on what he knew, than Bulat did.

The librarian had other issues with the story, however. The whole thing sounded like a fun-house-mirror version of the Arthur-Guinevere-Launcelot triangle, complete with analogues of Merlin and Morgaine in Koschei and Yaga.

"I have not finished the story, okay?" Bulat said. He got to his feet and slid his sword out of its scabbard. A metallic shriek echoed through the library as he did so. "You see, Koschei's immortality did not just go away." He then sliced into his left arm with the sword.

Buffy and Faith both got to their feet and said, "Hey!" but Giles had already worked it out. "Of course," he said, even as the bloody gash on Bulat's left arm stopped bleeding almost immediately. "By killing Koschei, you made yourself immortal."

"Yes. I went back to Baba Yaga after I realized what had happened. She laughed at me and said that I was as big a fool as Koschei was. The egg did not contain Koschei's death, it contained the spell that made him immortal. By striking him with the egg, I simply transferred the spell to me. It cannot be broken, merely transferred." He wiped away the blood with his hand, which was sloppy work, but he got rid of enough of it to show that the skin was smooth where he'd sliced it open only moments before. "She told me that she gave me the chance to stop him because she thought that immortality was better off in a dullard such as myself."

Buffy shook her head. "That certainly sounds like the lady we met today."

"She lied to me to stop Koschei. She has probably lied to you."

Faith said, "Well, for starters, she said that *she* killed Koschei."

Bulat gestured at Faith. "See? I risked everything to kill him, and she takes the credit."

"All right, fine," Buffy said, "so you got screwed by Baba Yaga. But it was all thanks to your putting Ivan and Vasilisa together."

Lowering his head, Bulat said, "I only wished my Vasilisa to be happy."

Giles, who still wasn't entirely convinced that Bulat was telling the whole truth despite the notable similarities between his narrative and the extant tales, said, "Yes, I can see that altruism was *all* that was on your mind."

In a quiet tone Bulat said, "I do not appreciate your implication."

"Oh come *on*," Faith said. "You expect us to believe it wasn't so you could keep your honey close by?"

"And that's another thing." Buffy jumped up from her chair and approached Bulat. "Why did Ivan free you, anyhow? Seems a little sudden to me."

"It does not matter," Bulat said quickly. "The point is, Koschei the Deathless had taken Vasilisa, and the only way to rescue her was to go to another wielder of magic."

"Who isn't to be trusted," Buffy said snippily.

"Yes, well," Bulat said with a sheepish smile, "I did not know that at the time. . . ."

Buffy said, "I think it does matter why Ivan freed you."

"Seems obvious to me," Faith said with a shrug. "Ivan had the hots for him."

Giles's eyes widened, but as soon as Faith said it, it all fell into place. "Of course—his lack of interest in marrying until he absolutely had to, his instantly freeing a man of your, ah, obvious good looks . . ."

"*Real* obvious," Faith said that with a feral grin.

That prompted a bow from Bulat. "Thank you."

"However," Giles said while straightening his tie, "whilst I appreciate your telling us this, I'm afraid that I must raise one rather important point."

"Yes?"

"Can you stop Koschei from being resurrected?"

At first Bulat said nothing, just stared ahead with those captivating blue eyes of his. "I cannot, no."

Giles added, "Given that she went to such lengths to have him killed once already, I imagine that she would be equally motivated now."

"Yes, that is true." Bulat, Giles couldn't help but notice, said those words with the utmost reluctance.

"Then I'm afraid there's very little different that we can do. At the moment, Baba Yaga is our best hope of preventing Koschei's resurrection. I've been reading up on the *Vozrozhdeniye*, and I've confirmed that at least a hundred lives must be sacrificed in order to bring about the resurrection."

Buffy's eyes widened. "A *hundred*?"

"Yes. Resurrection is a difficult business, and it gets more so the further one gets from the original death. With centuries having passed . . ."

"Okay," Bulat said, "I understand. But Baba Yaga is *not* to be trusted!"

"We *get* that," Buffy said. "Look, do you plan on sticking around?"

"I'm sorry?"

Closing her eyes, Buffy let out a breath and then opened them. "Are you staying in Sunnydale?"

"I can do this, yes."

"Good. Tomorrow's Friday. After school, and all through the weekend, Yaga's gonna be here, giving Willow a crash course in necromancy."

"Who is Willow?"

"She is studying to be a witch," Giles said. "Yaga has agreed to take her on—temporarily, I might add—as an apprentice until Koschei's resurrection. Her instruction is happening here so it may be under my supervision. If you wish to observe and keep Yaga honest, I certainly would have no objection."

Bulat nodded. "Okay. Good. Thank you—all of you. You will not regret having the good right arm of Bulat the Brave. And I will stop Baba Yaga from doing anything she should not."

With that, he resheathed his sword and strode out of the library.

Buffy looked at Faith. "What do you think?"

"Nice abs. Good butt."

Chuckling, Buffy said, "I meant about what he said."

Faith shrugged. "Nothin'. I didn't trust that crazy Russian bitch before, so it's not like some himbo's gonna make all that much diff. And I don't trust *him,* either. But he's wicked good in a fight, and that may come in handy."

Giles said, "I, too, do not trust him, but under the circumstances I believe it would be best to subscribe to the adage regarding keeping one's friends close and one's enemies closer."

"We don't know that he's an enemy," Buffy said. "But you're right, we don't know that he's a friend, either."

"Still," Giles said, "someone who is, ah, 'wicked good' in a fight could be useful. Especially since we'll be without Angel for this."

That got Buffy's attention. She walked over to Giles, a look of deep concern on her face. "What're you talking about?"

"Er, well, Yaga said it herself: She can control dead things, including vampires. Angel would be subject to her control. We cannot risk his being in proximity to her. In fact, it might be wise of you to inform him of this the next time you see him."

"I . . ." Buffy hesitated, looking down at the floor.

Giles said, "It's all right, Buffy," even though it wasn't. Buffy had lied about—or at the very least, neglected to mention—Angel's return from whatever hell dimension she'd sent him to during the Acathla affair, and then promised she wouldn't see him again shortly before she proceeded to spend most of her spare time with him. The more they saw each other, the greater the risk that Angel would have a moment of true happiness, reverting him to his soulless, vampiric self.

Not that Giles considered it likely that a vampire who'd been stabbed by the girl he loved and sent to a hell dimension for who-knew-how-long (time moved more slowly in the nether realms) was likely to feel any kind of happiness, true or otherwise, but Giles wasn't especially comfortable with the risk. The last time Angel lost his soul, he'd killed Jenny Calendar— a woman who had come to mean a great deal to Giles—and followed that up with some rather sadistic torturing of Giles himself, resulting in wounds that made his recent encounter with the denizens of the Hellmouth look like a comparative walk in the park.

Still, Buffy was eighteen years old, and he was no longer her Watcher. It wasn't his place to say, *No, you may not see the man who nearly destroyed my life.*

To her credit, Buffy realized this. *Not enough to not see him, but enough to feel bad about it.* Giles wondered if that helped or not. If he were honest with himself, the answer was "not"—but that wouldn't stop him from letting her make her own decisions. Leaving aside any other considerations, telling Buffy she could no longer do something was a surefire way to get her to keep doing it. . . .

Putting her hand to her injured wrist, Faith said, "Well, if that's it, I got a bottle of painkillers at home with my name on it. See you tomorrow, B?"

Buffy nodded.

After Faith left, Buffy looked up at the librarian. "Giles, I know how you feel about Angel, but he *did* just help us save the world."

"I know," Giles said. "And his work is appreciated."

"Fine." Buffy rolled her eyes and started for the door. "I'll let him know you gave him a satisfactory report."

"Buffy!"

She stopped.

"Please understand that the situation with Angel—"

Holding up a hand, Buffy turned and said, "No, it's okay, Giles. I'm sorry. I'm not being fair to you. Or to me, or to him. It's not like we can actually *have* a real relationship, 'cause he'll turn into the big bad wolf again, and it's not like we can just be friends."

Giles nodded. He'd seen the intensity of the passion that Buffy and Angel had for each other. That wasn't the sort of fire that could dim into the warm glow of friendship—it could only burn brighter, or consume itself. *One could argue that, with the two of them, it's already done both.*

In a quiet voice he said, "Do what you have to, Buffy. See you tomorrow."

She nodded and left.

A few minutes later, Giles shut down the library and did likewise. He needed a good night's sleep. He had the feeling it was going to be a very long weekend.

"Hey, Gi— Oh, my *God*, what is that *smell*?"

Buffy found herself gagging as she said those words upon entering the library on Saturday afternoon. Oz, Giles, and Cordelia, of all people, were sitting around the table, surrounded by a huge pile of books and scrolls and papyrus and whatever else Giles had dug out of his archives.

Oz curled his lip. "The sweet smell of success, if you're trying to be a necromancer's apprentice."

Cordelia shivered. "It makes Willow's usual spice rack smell like Chanel No. 5."

"Baba Yaga and Willow are in my office," Giles said, "along with Bulat."

"And how's that going?" Buffy asked as she approached the table.

That question was answered by the sound of shattering glass and a small scream from Willow, followed by a stream of invective in a high-pitched voice, all coming from Giles's office. Buffy didn't recognize the language, but she assumed it to be Russian.

Giles sighed. "About as you'd expect, I'd say."

Buffy shook her head. Yaga had not reacted at all to Bulat's presence, which had annoyed the swordsman, to say the least. Buffy suspected that he had wanted her to get all outrage-y, but all she did was shrug and start instructing Willow in the wild and wacky ways of necromancy.

As the argument in the office continued, Buffy looked at Cordelia. "What brings you here on a Saturday?"

Again, Cordelia shivered. "My mother's throwing one of her garden parties and, despite my begging and pleading, she invited her twin brothers-in-law."

Cordelia had, naturally, spoken as if everyone in the world should know the significance of her twin uncles attending a garden party. "And the problem is?"

"If I want to be hit on, I'll go to the Bronze with people born *after* 1980, not sit at home with two guys born in 1950."

Buffy nodded. "Got it."

"I swear, nothing in the *world* is as lame as having two aging hippies drooling on your blouse. So when Oz said you guys were doing your nerd thing today, I came with. Even with Obsession for Zombies back there, it sounded like a better offer."

"Really, I got it, Cordy." Buffy looked at Giles. "So, anything for a Slayer to—"

"I demand that this buffoon be sent away."

Buffy turned to see Yaga standing in the doorway to Giles's office, hands on hips, looking, Buffy thought, just like a substitute teacher who was trying to impose discipline on a class that didn't take her at all seriously because she was a sub.

"*I* am a buffoon?" Bulat said as he came out of the office behind her. "I did not knock the jar over, *you* did, Grandmother."

Behind *him*, Willow was just barely visible, and Buffy could see she was stricken.

Yaga whirled on him. "You always were an imbecile, and immortality has only made you *more* so!"

"That's *enough*!" Buffy yelled. They both stopped and turned to look at her. "That's better. What happened?"

They both started talking at once, only occasionally in English, and Buffy had to yell again. "Hold it! Forget it, I don't wanna know what happened. Just fix it and do what you have to do to stop Koschei."

"I am *trying*, but this idiot is interfering," Yaga said. "I insist he be sent away."

"I go *nowhere*, Grandmother. You made a fool of me once, I will not let you do it to these good people."

Yaga tittered again. "I never made a fool of you, young Bulat. Nature did that long before you came to me."

Bulat snarled and his hand went to his sword hilt, but Buffy said, "Bulat!"

After a second, Bulat's hand fell to his side.

"Well done, Slayer," Yaga said. "Since you have tamed him, you may—"

"No one tames Bulat the Brave!" His hand went to his sword hilt again.

Yaga went on as if Bulat had not spoken. "—You may order him to be gone until he is needed."

Buffy smiled sweetly. "Sorry. If you want him gone, you'll have to do it yourself. And I'm willing to bet that you can't. Just like you couldn't stop Koschei."

The look on Yaga's face was all Buffy needed to confirm that her guess was right. She went on: "You needed Bulat to stop Koschei back then because you couldn't do anything to whoever had that immortality spell—which means you can't hurt him now. So if you want him gone, do it yourself. And if you can't—then it doesn't matter that Faith and I can't harm you, because *he* can."

The library was very silent for several seconds. For a few moments, Buffy was worried that it might have been a tactical error to piss off an immortal sorceress.

But then Yaga simply said, "I must go replace the items this oaf has destroyed with his clumsiness. I will be back in one hour." She looked at Bulat. "Try not to break anything *else*. I have much to teach this young woman, and very little time to do it." Then she looked at Willow and smiled. "Thankfully, she is a very quick study. She would make a fine permanent apprentice."

Giles stepped forward. "Do not even *consider*—"

Yaga waved an arm. "Oh, do not fret, Mr. Giles, I have no interest in taking on an unwilling student for anything other than an emergency. I prefer my apprentices to come to me voluntarily. Besides—*you* would make a far more fitting student."

With that, she turned on her heel and left the library. Giles started furiously polishing his glasses. *He's going to wear them down to nothing by the time this is over*, Buffy thought.

Bulat broke into a wide grin. "That was very enjoyable. Thank you, Buffy Summers, you have given me wonderful experience: humiliating Baba Yaga."

"No problem," Buffy said with a chuckle. She then turned to her best friend. "You okay, Will?"

Willow nodded quickly. "I'm fine. It was just getting a little awkward in there."

"I am sorry for that, Willow Rosenberg," Bulat said. "But Baba Yaga is not to be—"

"—trusted. We heard you the *first* thousand times," Buffy said quickly.

Willow smiled. "But it's all right. I'm learning all kinds of new stuff. Okay, mostly icky new stuff, but I'm starting to understand the process a little more, too."

"Just be careful, okay?"

"Always," Willow said.

Somehow, that didn't make Buffy feel better. *At least we've got Bulat to keep Yaga honest.*

Then something occurred to Buffy. "How come Xander's not here?"

"How come anyone cares?" Cordelia muttered.

Ignoring her, Buffy said, "I've hardly seen him at all since the last apocalypse."

Oz said, "I called him this morning. His dad said he was out."

"He didn't say where?" Buffy asked.

Willow smiled. "Mr. Harris isn't much for conversation. You're lucky if you get a 'hello' when he picks up the phone."

"I didn't," Oz said. "It was more like a monosyllabic grunt."

Buffy didn't like the sound of this. "It's not like him to bail on research."

"Right, 'cause then who'd get the donuts?" Cordelia asked.

Again, ignoring Cordelia—after two-and-a-half years, it had become a survival skill—Buffy said, "Maybe I'll stop by his house, see if I can get a more detailed answer."

"We have somewhat more pressing concerns," Giles said. "We've learned a bit more about Koschei, and none of it is good."

"Of course," Bulat said. "He is an evil sorcerer. What could be good?"

"We've also confirmed the first two stages of the *Vozrozhdeniye*. The first, as we established, is the disappearance of a freshly killed body with an undamaged face. Yaga has added that it is likely to be that of a good-looking young man, as Koschei was rather vain."

"It comes of living forever when everyone around you dies," Bulat said in unusually hushed tones. "You either become vain or go mad. Or both."

Buffy thought about Angel, who'd been alive for over two hundred years—which was only a portion of how long Bulat and Yaga had been immortal. She found she couldn't even wrap her mind around the idea. Shaking her head, she asked, "What's the second step?"

Giles removed his glasses. "Disappearances. It isn't simply that a hundred or so people must die, but they must all be gathered together and rendered insensate."

"Rendered insensate how?"

Giles, Cordelia, and Oz all looked at each other. Oz finally said, "We're still workin' on that."

"It is difficult to find anything useful," Giles added. "Normally, I would simply send for more material on Eastern Europe and Asia, but—"

"The Watchers' Council's not returning your phone calls?" Buffy sighed. "You know, I keep thinking it's not possible to hate those guys more, and then they go and raise the bar again."

"Be that as it may, we're continuing to search. However, another pair of eyes would be useful."

Declining to take the hint Giles was making, Buffy headed exitward. "Then I'd better seriously try to find Xander. Besides, if I keep breathing through my mouth, I'm gonna hyperventilate. See you later!"

Buffy dashed out before anyone could stop her. The smell really *was* starting to get to her. *Cordy's uncles must be really bad news if she's putting up with that on a Saturday.* But even if the library had smelled like its usual musty self, Buffy had too much nervous energy to just sit there and read—or sit at home, for that matter, which was why she had gone to the school to check in.

So a Xander hunt would be just the thing to keep her occupied.

At least that was what she told herself in her head. Her feet, however, apparently of their own accord, took her to the mansion.

It was midday. The Southern California sun was shining brightly in the partly cloudy sky, reflecting off the mansion's stonework to make it shine like a beacon.

She knew Angel was inside—asleep, most likely, it being midday and all. He had probably been inside the twelve times she'd come here since Thursday but been too afraid to enter.

Why are you suddenly so chicken? she admonished herself. *You're just coming to visit him like you've done a thousand times before.* But she knew what was causing her to hesitate. *I've never had to tell him that I can't use him in a fight. Even when I've tried to break it off with him, like after Spike came to town, I've never said I didn't need him.*

She stood at the bottom of the hill for five full minutes, not moving a muscle, neither heading toward the mansion nor walking away.

I'll come back tonight when I know he's awake.

Content with the rationalization—the latest in a series—she turned and ran in the direction of the Harris house.

Seven hours later, Buffy found herself right back in the same spot. It had gotten dark, and a light breeze was blowing in off the ocean, sending the parts of Buffy's blond hair that weren't tied back flying about. Even in February, the weather in Southern California was close to perfect. Buffy could never understand why anyone would willingly live in a place with winter. Of course, this past Christmas, something—the forces of good, of order, the powers that be, whatever it was—had hit Sunnydale with a snowstorm to save Angel. . . .

Why can't I go in there? She had been trying to distract herself from Angel, but thinking about the snowstorm brought her brain right back to him.

"I thought you were the one who had to invite me in, not the other way around."

Whirling around, Buffy saw Angel had snuck up on her. Getting her heartbeat back under control, she said, "I *wish* you wouldn't do that."

He smiled. "Three years, I keep hoping you'll hear me."

"No, you don't. You like being all sneaky and mysterious."

The smile fell. "Not with you."

He lifted his hand. Buffy started to lean her cheek into it, then quickly pulled back. "I—I can't do this."

"We're not doing anything," Angel whispered.

Buffy deliberately took a step back. "I know, and we can't. Look, I can't—" She broke off.

"Can't what?"

She looked up at him. He was dressed in his usual getup: duster, white shirt, slacks. *He looks hot, dammit.* As entertaining as it was to stare at Bulat's biceps, it was Angel who represented everything that was attractive to her. She had felt a pull toward him the first time she saw him, and she felt it now.

Taking a breath and forcing herself to look away, she said, "I can't ask you to help me on this one. Someone's trying to resurrect some old Russian sorcerer, and one of the people helping us—"

"Baba Yaga. I know."

Now she looked back at him, and there was less longing and more anger. "How do you *do* that?"

Angel stepped back as if she'd hit him. "Do what?"

"You always—always *know* stuff!" Buffy threw up her arms in frustration and started pacing. "Giles and Willow and the others, they spend hours doing research, I beat Willy to a pulp to get more info, and then I come here, and you *know* everything already!"

Contritely, Angel said, "I have my own sources—and a lot of them wouldn't talk to Giles. And I already knew about the house on chicken legs."

"I guess it's not your fault." Buffy looked down at the pavement, then back up at Angel. He had his most endearing puppy-dog expression on his face, and Buffy desperately wanted to kiss him and make it all better.

Except too much of that will make him worse . . .

Shaking the feeling off, she said, "If you know about Madam Chicken Legs, then you know why we need you to stay away."

"Believe me, every vamp in town knows about her—whether they want to or not."

Nodding, Buffy said, "Well, stay here, okay? Don't leave the mansion until this is all over. Please?"

Angel hesitated. Buffy understood why—he was a man of action, after all. It wasn't in him to just sit around when there was evil to be fought. It was an instinct they both shared. *No matter what we can't have, we'll always have the fight.*

Buffy just wished that was enough.

"Okay," he finally said. "Let me know when it's all over."

"It'll be soon. Giles's Russian scholar and Creepy Russian Lady both said that in a few days nobody will be able to resurrect this Deathless guy."

"Good. I'll see you on the other side, then."

Angel winced as soon as he said it, and Buffy felt her heart beat faster. She'd already lost him once—by her own hand, no less—and the idea of losing him again . . .

Don't think about it. Walk away. Fight the next fight. Deal with this later.

She wondered how much longer they'd be able to put this off before something had to happen. They just couldn't keep dancing around each other. . . .

Or maybe we can. I like dancing. Dancing is good.

So resolved, she headed toward home.

Chapter Eight

"**W**elcome, seniors!"

Willow Rosenberg was greatly relieved that it was the school guidance counselor, William "It's okay, call me Bill!" Powers, who was leading the Ring Day festivities, rather than Snyder. Two Snyder speeches in one week would have half the senior class slitting their wrists.

On the bright side, she thought, *now I know how to resurrect them if they do!*

It was a bad joke, and she was sorry she'd made it as soon as she thought it. Giles had been right about necromancy. What had fascinated Willow about magic was the way you worked with nature to mold the forces of the earth. Necromancy, though, wasn't really about that, it was about twisting the forces of earth and bending them to your will. She'd never been big on that sort of thing. In fact, Willow had gone through life with a very firm anti-bending-to-your-will bias.

Another problem with necromancy was that it seriously brought the stinky. It seemed like every ingredient needed to work with the dead was required to smell just as bad as a decomposing corpse. Willow had taken the longest shower of her life this morning in the hopes of getting the *eau de* dead people out of her skin and hair, but she still found herself surrounded by empty chairs at the Ring Day ceremony. Even her fellow aspiring mage Michael Czajak, who was used to smelly magical stuff, chose to sit with his Goth friends across the auditorium instead of with Willow.

Xander dashed in just as Mr. Powers had begun to speak, and sat next to Willow. "Sorry I'm late," he whispered. Then his nose crinkled. "Will? What've you been *eating*?"

"I've been doing spells," she whispered back, "which you'd know if you'd been around. Where've you *been*? Buffy went looking for you over the weekend, and Oz called you, and nobody could find you!"

"Been busy—but it's okay, it's just temporary."

Willow looked closely at Xander, and didn't like what she saw. He had bags under his very bloodshot eyes, and he looked like he had lost weight.

"What's only temporary?" she finally asked.

"Just a job my uncle got me."

"How did Rory get *you* a job? He can't even get himself one."

Xander shook his head. "Not Rory, Uncle Charlie."

Willow frowned. "The one with the hair on his nose?"

"Yup. Only guy I've ever met with more hair on his nose than on top of his head. He needed some help loading boxes these last couple of weeks while one of his guys was on vacation, and I needed a ring, so we did a trade."

Before Willow could ask Xander more about it, Mr. Powers finally finished his speech. Willow had no idea what it had been about—she caught words like "spirit" and "legacy" and other words she'd been hearing *way* too much over the past two weeks—but he'd finally moved on to the main event. "And now, when I call your name, please come forward and take your ring! Sally Aaronovitch."

The guidance counselor went through all the seniors present. When he got to the Cs, Willow was sure to sneer at Cordelia. *Okay, so she and Oz were both hurt when they showed up at the factory to rescue us and found Xander and me kissing. Oz forgave me, why can't she?*

Besides, she'd spent most of her life hating Cordelia. It was her default position.

Xander went up when he went through the Hs, and eventually he read off the Rs. Willow got into line behind Phil Rosen and worked her way to the stage.

Snyder was handing out the rings, which diminished the experience for Willow somewhat. Standing next to him was a tall man who had been introduced at the beginning of the ceremony as Alfredo LaManna of Avanas'ev Jewelry, the company providing the rings this year. This was new—Willow remembered that a place in the mall had made the rings in the past, but Snyder had apparently disliked their business practices. *Knowing Snyder, that meant they charged reasonable rates and treated their employees well.*

LaManna was much taller than Snyder—admittedly, not much of an accomplishment—with beady little eyes, a huge hook nose, and a big mole on his right cheek. He stood looming over the principal, and it made Willow nervous.

Phil took his ring and then Willow stepped up to the table.

Avanas'ev had gone all out, at least, actually providing small gray ring boxes to put the rings in. The boxes were open, a small tag on the inside of the lid indicating the new owner's name.

Snyder handed her ring over to her with the box open, as if he were proposing marriage. Willow shuddered.

"Rosenberg." Snyder was the only person Willow knew who could sneer a name.

Taking the ring, Willow quickly walked back to her seat. Xander had already put his on the ring finger of his right hand, and was holding it up and admiring it in the exact same manner as Willow's cousin Rachel had when she got engaged.

"Looks great, huh?" Xander said with a grin. "This is it, Will. This is my ticket to ride."

"That ring's a Beatles song?" she asked with a grin even as she took her own ring out of the box.

"Very funny. No, I mean, I'm tired of being the outcast, the pariah, the one who always gets picked last for everything. This here, this little band of silver, allows me to stand up and say, 'Hey—I *belong* here!'"

"Personally, I think you may have loaded one too many boxes."

Xander put his hand down and regarded Willow seriously. "Mock me if you must, Will, but I'm telling you, *this* is the key."

Grinning, Willow said, "Oh, I think I must mock you, yes. It's just a ring, Xander. I mean, it's nice and all, and I think it's great that you're getting one, but it's not like it's vital. I mean, Buffy isn't getting one, Oz isn't getting one."

Xander started looking around. "Yeah, I was wondering about the Buffster. Why isn't she being ringed?"

"Can't afford it. From what she said, the cleanup from her welcome-home party kinda drained her mom's finances."

Wincing, Xander said, "Ouchie. Doesn't homeowner's insurance cover that?"

"If it was a natural disaster, sure, but how do you put 'zombie attack' on your insurance claim?"

"Yeah, good point." Xander sighed. "Well, at least we have ours. Try it on, Will."

"Okay." Willow wasn't sure why she was hesitating to put hers on. She gazed down at it. The ring was thick and had a large multifaceted garnet in the middle, surrounded by the border of the school seal. On one side of the stone the number "99" was engraved; on the other side, a rendering of a razorback, the school's mascot. Inside the ring, the words WILLOW ROSENBERG were engraved, along with some kind of symbol. After a second, Willow recognized it as being the logo for Avanas'ev.

She slid it onto her right ring finger. As soon as it touched her skin, though, she felt a spark. "Ooh!"

"What is it?" Xander leaned forward, a concerned expression on his face.

Willow shook her head. "Nothing, just a little electric shock. Probably from the carpet."

After Lucy Zelenetzky got her ring, Snyder walked up to the podium.

Leaning back in the auditorium chair, Xander said, "Uh-oh. Get comfy, Will—the tedium is about to commence."

"I just wanted to say to all of you, congratulations on doing at least one thing right in your misbegotten careers as students. No matter what failures you'll endure in life, and I have every confidence that those failures will be legion, you can always hold up your right hand—even if it's to swear an oath in court during the criminal proceedings against you—and say that you went to Sunnydale High School and graduated in the Class of '99. Now all of you get out of here, we need to lock up."

Willow and Xander stood up, as did everyone else. Shaking her head, Willow said, "Nothing like a good inspirational speech."

Xander nodded. "And that was nothing like a good inspirational speech."

"C'mon, let's head to the library and we can remind everyone what you look like."

"What's happening?" Xander asked as they joined

the throng slowly moving down the aisle toward the exit.

"How up are you on Russian folklore?" Willow asked.

"I can safely say with impunity and malice afore-thought that I can definitely spell those two words."

"Oh." Willow let out a breath as they made it to the hallway. "This could take a while. . . ."

Buffy had spent the first half of Tuesday being apologized to by Xander. It had started out kinda cute, but after the fifteenth time had lost its appeal.

They were currently walking to the library together during their study hall, and he was trying to hit her with Apology #16.

"It's okay, Xander, really. Believe me, if Slaying wasn't in the way, I'd have done the same thing to get a ring. So you can just wear your ring for both of us," Buffy said.

Xander broke into a grin. "Okay, fair enough."

They entered the library to see Willow sitting at the table, in front of her laptop. "Buffy! Hey, you're gonna wanna see this."

Buffy walked over to the table, Xander trailing behind her.

"I'm surprised you're not in the back room with Yaga making with the death magic," Xander said.

Giles spoke up. "I thought it best not to have such magicks being practiced during school hours. The stench alone—"

"Fair point," Buffy said as she stood behind Willow. "So, what do I wanna see?" The laptop screen showed yet another coroner's report.

"This is just a prelim, but—"

Xander interrupted. "'Prelim'? The Willster, pickin' up the coroner lingo."

"Actually," Willow said with a grin of her own, "the preferred term is 'medical examiner,' not 'coroner.'"

"My bad."

"What's the report?" Buffy asked. She had a feeling she knew what it was already.

Willow pointed at the screen. "This is Peter Burton. Twenty-seven years old, assistant manager at Doublemeat Palace."

Xander said, "Let me guess, he died from eating the food?"

"No, a heart attack. The report says he had a history of heart trouble. And he's not bad looking. That's not the important part, though." She clicked on another window. "This is a missing body report, and the tag number matches."

Buffy straightened up. "So now we have a missing body."

Willow nodded.

"We sure this isn't a vamp?" Xander asked. "It's not like it's the first body to go missing from the freezer in this town."

"I checked the report," Willow said. "No bite marks. His body was pristine."

"Which makes it ideal," Giles said. "Based on what we know of the *Vozrozhdeniye*, the late Mr. Burton is likely to be the new receptacle for Koschei."

Buffy nodded. "All right. After school, Faith and I'll hit the streets, see if we can find out who's playing Invasion of the Body Snatchers."

"Need a hand?" Xander asked. "I can threaten to beat people up with my big new class ring."

Chuckling, Buffy said, "That's okay. Why don't you stay here and make with the research?"

"I fear that may be fruitless," Giles said. "Over the weekend we exhausted my own library—both here and at home—and the Council continues to not return my phone calls. I'm afraid that we know all that there is to know about the situation, barring some new intelligence." He paused, getting that thoughtful Watcher look of his. "On the other hand, a fresh set of eyes might be useful, if you wouldn't mind, Xander?"

"No problemo, muchacho. You know me, always willing to help out in a crunch, whether you need me or not."

"Thanks, Xander. That means a lot." And Buffy meant it. They had shunted Xander to the side a bit during the whole Sisterhood of Jhe thing, and Buffy had feared that they had gone a little too far. She had no regrets about keeping Xander out of harm's way. Had it been possible, she would have done the same with Giles and Willow, but their magical skills and knowledge were necessary. It had been hard enough for Buffy, Angel, and Faith, and they were built for apocalyptic fighting.

Leaving Xander to the research, Buffy sat down with her chemistry homework. *No sense in giving Snyder an excuse to keep my diploma from me at the end of the semester . . .*

Chapter Nine

Lesley Anton choked down her Cheerios while her mother babbled on.

It was the same thing every morning, and it drove Lesley nuts. Mother wouldn't let her eat anything other than Cheerios, and she only bought one-percent milk. Lesley would as soon eat cardboard as eat Cheerios willingly, and one-percent milk tasted like rancid water to her. But skipping breakfast would just mean a lecture about the most important meal of the day, which Mother had lifted right from television.

The lecture would, of course, mean a break from the talk about work. Mother worked as a receptionist for a doctor, and every morning Lesley got to hear about all the crazy patients Dr. Price had that day. Mother worked from one to nine, so Lesley didn't have these conversations over dinner—Lesley's dinners were generally from the frozen-foods section of the supermarket—because Mother got home too late. So instead Lesley got it first thing in the morning.

At least the stories were occasionally entertaining, like that guy who had his cell phone antenna stuck up his nose and refused to go to the emergency room because it was too embarrassing, or the lady who insisted that aliens were talking to her through the staples they used for her surgery.

Today was pretty boring, though, and Lesley just wanted it over. So she ate her cereal faster, trying not to gag the whole time, in the hopes that she could get out of there.

As soon as she scooped the last three Cheerios into her mouth, she got up and put the bowl in the sink.

"All done?" Mother asked.

"Just about," Lesley said, gulping down the last of her orange juice—the only part of breakfast she liked, especially since Mother always got the pulpy kind. "Hey, I'm gonna walk to school today, okay?"

Why did I say that?

Mother looked as surprised as Lesley felt. "Okay, baby, if that's what you want."

"Yeah, it's a nice day, and I feel like stretching my legs."

No it isn't a nice day! I hate stretching my legs! What's wrong with me? But Lesley couldn't stop herself from saying the words.

Shrugging, Mother said, "Sure." She walked up to Lesley and gave her a kiss on the cheek. "You be good and you be careful, okay? Good and careful."

"*Yes*, Mother." That she had no trouble saying—it was what she always said when Mother gave her good-and-careful litany.

Lesley hauled her backpack up from its place next to the front door and walked out. "Bye!"

Her legs seemed to be moving of their own volition. Lesley couldn't stop herself, even though she wanted—*desperately* wanted—to turn around and go back to the house and make Mother drive her to school. *What's happening to me?*

To make matters worse, when she left the house, she turned left. Sunnydale High was twelve blocks to the *right*. Why was she walking toward the warehouse district?

As she walked, her newly acquired school ring shot a small burst of static electricity into her right ring finger. . . .

Cordelia Chase took her morning latte from Lupe. At least she tried to—Lupe's hands were all shaky.

"Excuse me?" she said. "The foam's gonna get on the table." The foam from the steamed skim milk was Cordelia's favorite part. Without that, she might as well just drink regular coffee like her father, and why would she do *that*?

"I'm sorry, Miss Chase." Lupe's accent was really thick this morning, which meant she was in one of her moods. Cordelia hoped she was still on the right meds. "I'm not feeling well today."

Rolling her eyes as she sipped her latte, Cordelia thought, *Great, she's going to give us all whatever illness she's picked up again.* "If you're not feeling well, take a couple hours off and go see a doctor."

Lupe was buttering Cordelia's croissant with fat-free spread. "You sure, Miss Chase?"

"Completely." Cordelia took the croissant from Lupe and took a bite. It was flaky and warm and wonderful, with the spread just dripping enough. "Trust me, Lupe, I don't want anything to happen to you. You're the only person who knows how to prepare a croissant."

That got a small smile out of Lupe. "Thank you, Miss Chase." She said that with less of an accent.

"Now, if you could just make the beds right. You always put the wrong pillow on top."

The accent came back full force. "I'm so sorry, Miss Chase, I try to remember to put feather pillow on top. I always get mixed up with Mrs. Chase, who wants the down pillow on top."

"It shouldn't be *that* hard to tell us apart, Lupe. I'm the one who *hasn't* botoxed her lips within an inch of her life and who has her natural hair color."

"Of course, Miss Chase. Here are your medications." She was holding out two white pills.

Cordelia was about to object that she didn't need the meds even as she reached for them, but the ache that that motion put in her side convinced her otherwise. She popped the pills in her mouth and washed them down with the last of the latte.

"You need anything else?"

"A boy who doesn't suck and a side that doesn't ache."

Lupe smiled. "I will see what I can do." Then she left the kitchen.

Cordelia finished her croissant in peace. The pain from being impaled on a metal rod was actually mostly gone, but as long as there was even the slightest ache, Cordelia intended to down the Darvocet. Nothing was standing between her and a pain-free existence, and every twinge just reminded her of Xander and Willow smooching in the factory while she and Oz risked their lives to rescue them. . . .

She banished the thought. Sooner or later, the right guy would come along. Until then, she was going to be carefree and fancy-free and whatever other kind of free she could think of.

So determined, she grabbed her books off the kitchen table and walked out the door. For some reason, though, she headed west on Oxford Drive instead of to the garage where her car was. *What's going on?* She couldn't make her feet move in the opposite direction.

As she wondered what stupid Hellmouth thing was happening *this* time, her school ring sent a shock through her right ring finger. . . .

Percy West threw the basketball toward the hoop over the garage.

It went in with a satisfying swoosh. *Nothin' but net.*

Jogging forward, he snagged the ball as it bounced off the garage door, then whirled around and took another shot.

It bounced off the garage wall, hit the rim, then fell to the ground.

Dammit. He chased the ball down again. He needed to be able to make that shot.

From the spot in the driveway that Percy figured was about the same as the three-point line, he jumped and shot.

Swoosh. *All right!*

Percy chased the ball down and was about to jump for another shot when he was surprised by a car horn.

"Dude, let's *go*!"

Turning around as the ball bounced into the front yard, Percy saw Hogan Marin's Chevy pull up.

Shaking his head and laughing, Percy started jogging toward the car. "Dude, you have *got* to get a real car."

"When the scholarship money comes pouring in, you'll be the first to sit in the passenger seat of my Porsche." Hogan grinned. "Well, okay, second. First is gonna be Harmony."

"Dude, forget it—she's into *me*."

"You wish. C'mon, get in. Uh, wait."

Percy was just about to open the passenger door. "What?"

"Schoolbooks?"

For a second, Percy just stared blankly at Hogan. It wasn't like he had actually *done* his homework or anything, but teachers got all mad when you showed up without books, so he ran back to the garage, grabbed his bookbag—he'd left it lying by the garage door— and then jogged back to the Chevy.

Right after he got in, Hogan pulled out and drove down Johnson Avenue. Something seemed wrong to Percy—shouldn't they have been driving down Cannon Street?—but he didn't worry about it.

As Hogan drove, Percy felt a stab of pain in his right ring finger. . . .

Harmony Kendall decided that now was the time to finally look at that poem she was supposed to read for English class. After all, class was only in a couple of hours, and sometimes Mr. Bruner called on her. She wasn't sure *why* he called on her; it's not like any answer she ever gave was what he wanted to hear. It was like he had it in for her or something.

The more she thought about it, the more she thought it was a bad idea to waste valuable hours of her life going through all fourteen lines of some dumb poem about a loser named Ozzy Mandias. Mr. Bruner was just going to put her on the spot and call her stupid in class again, like he did last month. Harmony was just going to have to prove him right!

She slammed the poetry textbook shut, dropped it onto the pile of books with a satisfying thump, then went to the bathroom to check her makeup for the seventh time before going to school.

Once she got to her car, she checked her makeup in the rearview for the eighth time, then pulled out and started driving toward the warehouse district. She wasn't entirely sure why she was going that way instead of toward school, but there was probably a good reason for it, so Harmony didn't think about it all that much.

As she drove, she noticed a tingle in her right ring finger. . . .

Xander Harris figured if he tiptoed out the door, he'd be able to avoid his parents.

It worked about 80 percent of the time. Unfortunately, today he was the victim of the 20 percent failure rate.

"Off to school?" Dad asked as he exited the bathroom just as Xander passed it.

Xander sighed. He had thought it was Mom in there, which would have meant the door would have remained closed for at least another half hour. "Yeah. Gotta road test the ring." He held up his right hand for effect.

"Then you've got work afterward, right?"

Blinking, Xander said, "Uh, no. That's done with. Uncle Charlie only needed me until Ryon came back from vacation, and he's back in today."

"Too bad—that job was the brightest thing you ever did." Dad looked down at Xander's right hand. "Kind of a waste to spend all your paychecks on that, you ask me. But then, it's not like you have a girlfriend to spend it on, and better a class ring than those stupid comic books." He looked at his watch. "I'm late for work."

With that, Dad stomped downstairs. "Where the hell's my coffee?" he bellowed as he entered the kitchen.

Xander counted to ten, then went downstairs also, being sure to bypass the kitchen, where Dad was explaining to Mom in words of four letters about how and where he expected his morning coffee. As usual, he was explaining at such a loud volume that Giles could probably make out every syllable from the Sunnydale High library three miles away. *Heck, satellites are probably picking it up from orbit.*

Opening the door, Xander started walking toward the warehouse district.

Okay, this is wrong. I should be going to Uncle Rory's car. I still have it for another week, and I want to take it to school. I even left early so I could get a good parking space before the rich kids show up and take two spaces with their Camaros.

But he kept walking. He tried to change direction, but he couldn't even turn his head to look behind him.

Oh, wow, do I not like this. Xander had been possessed before, and given who he hung around with and how he spent his days—and, more to the point, his nights—he suspected that he'd be possessed again in the future, and as a result, he recognized the signs.

Unfortunately, that didn't do him a lick of good. His feet kept on ambulating in the opposite direction from the school.

I have a bad feeling about this.

As he walked, his right ring finger started to throb. . . .

Chapter Ten

"Giles, something *really* weird's going on."

Buffy had barely walked through the library doors as when she spoke to Giles, who looked at her with his patented British Look of Befuddlement. "Buffy? Shouldn't you be in your history class?"

"Mr. Beech canceled it, mostly 'cause me and Freddy Iverson were the only people in class. Freddy probably went off to write an editorial about it."

"That is peculiar."

Buffy assumed he meant it was peculiar that there were only two people in European History, not that Freddy would write an editorial for the *Sunnydale High Sentinel*.

She walked up to the main desk, behind which Giles was standing and sorting through returned books. "It gets peculiarer. There are only, like, ten people in the whole senior class here. Homeroom was a wasteland. And Xander and Cordelia aren't in, either. I haven't seen Willow yet, and I definitely haven't seen a single class ring today."

Giles stopped in mid-sort. "All the seniors who are out are the ones who got rings?"

"Yup."

"This bodes ill. I take it you had no luck locating the remains of the late Mr. Burton?"

"Nope. Faith and I staked a couple vamps, but it was pretty run-of-the-mill. What's got me—"

Before Buffy could say what had gotten her, Willow and Oz entered the library. "Hi, Buffy! Class was canceled."

Oz added, "The day's kinda lacking in seniors."

"So much for that theory," Buffy muttered.

"What theory?" Willow asked.

Buffy quickly summed it up, finishing with: "But you have your ring."

"Well, yeah." Willow looked down at her right hand. "But come to think of it, I don't remember anyone having rings in homeroom, either." She brightened. "No, wait, Michael did!"

"I don't like this. Will, can you and Oz go to Xander's place and find out where he went this morning? I'll go to Cordelia's."

Nodding, Oz said, "We're on it."

As they left, Giles said, "Be careful, Buffy."

She grinned. "I'm only going to talk to Cordy's parents, Giles. It's not like I'm going after a demon in his lair."

"Think about what they must be like to have raised her."

Buffy considered. "Yeah, okay, good point. Maybe I should bring the machete."

Giles actually smiled at that. "I wouldn't go that far, but be wary. If nothing else, parents tend to get overprotective when something happens to their children, and if Koschei's involved, that might put them in harm's way as well."

Remembering how half the adults in Sunnydale acted the last time a fairy tale had come to life—which ended up with Buffy, Willow, and Amy tied to stakes and about to be Joan of Arc'd by their own parents—Buffy said, "I'll be careful."

Half an hour later, Buffy reentered the library. Willow and Oz—who'd had the advantage of Oz's van—were already back. Michael was also present, dressed in his usual Goth Poster Child uniform: all-black regalia, moussed-up hair, and eyeliner.

"No luck at the Chase residence. I didn't have to worry about spooking the parents, but I did talk to the maid. Cordy left for school this morning after a latte and a croissant, like usual."

"So did Xander, according to his mom," Willow said.

"Minus the latte and croissant," Oz added.

"However, there is a wrinkle," Giles said. "Young Michael here and Willow are the only seniors who are present who obtained rings last night."

"And I got gypped," Michael put in. "Look at this." He was holding out his ring.

Buffy took it and noticed that the gold ring had a chip on the band. Under the chip was silver, not gold.

She looked up. "Gold-plated?"

"So it would seem," Giles said.

"My dad's gonna be pissed," Michael said. His voice went deeper. "'For once in your life, you'll do something that makes me happy,' he said. That's why he paid more for the gold—he said he wanted *something* he could show the rest of the family." He smiled, his eyeliner-laden eyes crinkling up. "He hasn't shown them a recent picture."

After a knowing smile at Michael—she had her own issues of being an outcast, between burning down her last high school's gym and her parents' divorce—she looked at Willow. "Will, didn't you say that silver was better for spells?"

Nodding, Willow said, "Silver is better for conducting magic. Gold's too soft; it deadens it."

Buffy was about to say something to Giles when Yaga walked in. "The abductions have commenced, it seems."

"Indeed," Giles said. "We believe it has something to do with the class rings."

"Really?" Yaga raised an eyebrow. "May I see one, please?"

Since she had Michael's in hand already, Buffy handed it over to Yaga.

The sorceress examined it all around. "This is quite hideous. Why does it have a pig?"

"Mascot," Buffy said. "Can you tell us anything useful? We already know the school has lousy taste."

Yaga looked inside the ring, and said, "Ah, here it is. The symbol next to Mr. Czajak's name."

Willow said, "That's the logo of the jewelry company."

"It is more than that, Ms. Rosenberg, it is a sigil."

"Oh, dear," Giles said.

Buffy noticed Willow and Michael both frowning also. "A sigil is bad?"

"Not necessarily," Giles said. "A sigil is simply a mystical character used to channel magic."

"And this one channels a possession spell?" Buffy guessed.

"Very good, Ms. Summers," Yaga said, handing the ring back. "It is a very simple spell, but no less effective for that."

"Oooh!" Willow said, waving her arm up and down. "When I put the ring on, I felt a little jolt. I thought it was static electricity or something, but it was probably the spell, right?"

"Yes." Yaga looked at both Michael and Willow. "I assume, in your studies, you have cast protection spells?"

"They're pretty basic ones," Michael said, "but, yeah, sure. Who hasn't?"

"A basic one is all that is required," Yaga said, "because the spell in these rings is even simpler. It has taken all those wearing one, probably, to provide whatever necromancer is resurrecting Koschei with the souls he needs. A protection spell would keep the pair of you free of its influence. It would seem your classmates are less fortunate."

Willow muttered, "'One ring to bind them.'"

Buffy stared blankly at Willow. She was obviously quoting something—probably one of the poems she hadn't gotten around to reading for English class over the last year. She noticed similar blank looks on Oz and Michael's faces.

Rolling her eyes, Willow said, "*Lord of the Rings?* Tolkien?" She looked at Giles. "I can't believe nobody got that."

Oz said, "I don't think mainstream America's ever likely to get Tolkien references."

Yaga said, "Tell me, Ms. Rosenberg, was a representative from the jewelry company present at the ceremony last evening?"

The disappointed look from her face dissolving, Willow nodded.

"Describe him."

"Tall, skinny, hook nose, beady eyes—oh, and he had this mole—"

"Of course." Yaga sighed. "This is Alfredo."

"That was his name," Willow said. "Mr. Powers introduced him during the ceremony, Alfredo LaManna."

Buffy glared at Yaga. "You know him?"

"Remember the apprentice I mentioned who blew up a parking garage?"

"Alfredo LaManna?"

Yaga nodded.

"There you are!" an angry voice boomed.

Turning toward the door, Buffy saw Bulat the Brave storming in. He was carrying what looked like a poster tube on his back, which hid his sword. Buffy was grateful, as she didn't want to imagine Snyder's reaction to someone wandering around school grounds with a sword—especially on a day when most of the senior class was AWOL.

"You thought you could hide from me, Grand-mother, but I am not so easily shaken off!"

"I *know* I can hide from you, Bulat," Yaga said with a wicked smile, "and indeed I have on those occasions when I did not wish you around."

Bulat stepped forward. "Damn you, woman, you—"

"Enough!" Buffy yelled. "Bulat, it's good that you're here, anyhow. We need to find out where this Alfredo guy took all the seniors. Wherever they are, that's where Koschei's being resurrected. I'll get Faith to cover her neck of the woods, and—"

"There is no need for that," Yaga interrupted in an irritated tone. "I need no assistance to locate a former apprentice. Wait one moment."

Yaga then closed her eyes and crossed her hands just below the belt.

"Interesting," Giles said.

"What's she doing, Giles?" Buffy asked.

"That's a *makuso* meditation stance—usually used in Japanese martial arts, not Eastern European magic rituals."

Then Yaga opened her eyes. "That is . . . strange."

Oz said, "Pretty much par for the course, really."

To Willow Yaga said, "You saw Alfredo at the ring ceremony last evening, yes?"

"Yeah," Willow said with a nod. "I'm sure I did."

Michael said, "So did I."

"I can find no trace of him whatsoever."

Giles said, "Perhaps that wasn't your apprentice last night."

Yaga waved at Giles dismissively. "No, you do not understand, Mr. Giles. If he was anywhere in Sunnydale over the past decade, I would find his trail, and I know for a fact he *was* in Sunnydale up until seven years ago. Yet I find no trace of *that*. It means that he has masked his movements." She looked at Buffy. "This means he is in Sunnydale and is deliberately hiding from me."

"It seems," Bulat said with a sneer, "that you are not as all-powerful as you think you are, Grandmother."

"Oh, *do* stop calling me that," Yaga said irritably.

Ignoring both of them, Buffy said to Giles, "I'm going back to Plan A. Can you call Faith?"

"Of course," Giles said, moving toward the phone. "Bulat?"

Nodding, the swordsman said, "I will investigate the southern portions of the city."

"I can drive around, too," Oz said. "Couple of the other guys in the band got rings—I might pick up their scent."

Buffy's eyes went wide. "You can do that in human form?"

"If I know 'em well enough—Willow, the guys in the band, my parents."

Nodding, Buffy said, "Okay—icky, but okay. You've got nose patrol."

Michael got up. "I can go with him. I can't do much, but I might be able to help out."

"Sure," Buffy said. "And thanks." The last time Michael got mixed up in Scooby Gang business was during the Hansel-and-Gretl mess, and he had gotten his butt kicked. She hadn't expected the help but certainly wouldn't turn it down.

Yaga said, "I believe it is time Ms. Rosenberg and I put our hard work these last days to good use. The spell requires a certain amount of preparation. And I have other means of trying to locate the seniors, which I will employ."

"Fine." Buffy headed for the exit. With most of the seniors already absent, she doubted any teachers would miss her, Willow, Oz, and Michael.

Chapter Eleven

"Aw, c'mon, I just got the place fixed up!"

Buffy ignored Willy's words as she entered his bar. It had been a bad day, and it was turning into a bad night. She needed somebody to punch, and the denizens of Willy's bar were perfect candidates. She almost hoped they didn't know anything, so she could just beat them up.

She had spent the entire day searching the town trying to find *something* to indicate where the seniors had been taken, and had nothing but frustration to show for her trouble. Calling Giles via pay phone hadn't helped. According to Giles, Faith and Oz had both also checked in, each reporting a giant goose egg. Bulat hadn't been heard from at all, but Buffy was willing to bet he hadn't gotten the hang of the whole telephone thing.

One of the places Buffy had looked was the offices of Avanas'ev Jewelry. To her total lack of surprise, the offices were closed and cleaned out. The file cabinets were empty, the computers were gone, the storage room was empty, and there was a big OFFICE SPACE FOR RENT sign on the front window. *Alfredo didn't waste any time dropping* that *pretense. . . .*

As Buffy entered Willy's bar, she noticed two things. One was that Willy's arm was in a cast and he had a bandage on his head. He hadn't made it through the Sisterhood of Jhe's rampage in one piece either—in fact, Buffy had been the one to call the ambulance for him.

The other thing she noticed was that there were no vampires in the bar. The place was practically empty, and all she saw were a couple of demons, including one nursing a glass of what looked like rancid milk.

Walking up to the bar, which Willy was dabbing with a white rag, Buffy said, "You want to keep the place from being redecorated again, Willy, you'll answer my questions. Someone took most of the senior class of Sunnydale High for a resurrection ritual. I want to know where they are."

Now Willy started furiously cleaning the bar surface with the rag, refusing to look Buffy in the eyes. "How the hell should I know? I'm just a bartender."

Buffy rolled her eyes. "Right. You're just a bartender, and I'm just a senior struggling through chem class. Wanna try that one again, or you wanna go back to the hospital?"

Willy stopped cleaning and looked up at Buffy. "Look, I don't know nothin', okay? Really, I don't—I wish I did, too. Dunno if you noticed, but it's kinda dead here."

"It's usually dead here," Buffy said.

"No, it's usually *undead*, but I ain't been gettin' no vamps tonight. Got a keg fulla blood, and nobody's buyin'. And the ones I have seen?" Willy shuddered. "They're actin' capital-W weird, you know what I'm sayin'? Even Angel."

"Angel?" Buffy grabbed Willy by the lapels of his shirt—or where his lapels would've been if he wasn't wearing a white T-shirt—and yanked him forward, lifting him in the air and resting his stomach on the bar. "You saw Angel? *Today?*"

"Y-yeah, just—just after nightfall! C'mon, Slayer, put me down!"

"When did you see him?"

"I *told* you, just after nightfall! And he was actin' just as crazy as the others, all dazed."

Buffy let go of Willy, who stumbled to the floor behind the bar. Clambering to his feet, he started brushing off his shirt. "You wanna be more careful? Sheesh, lady stops an apocalypse, you'd think she'd be happier."

Ignoring him, Buffy turned on her heel and left the bar. She had a feeling she knew exactly who was making all the vampires in town act "all dazed." *And I intend to drop her chicken-legged hut on her head if she keeps this up. . . .*

"What the hell are you doing?"

Yaga did not look away from the three vampires

she was questioning as Buffy stormed into the library, and that served only to piss the Slayer off more. That, however, was as nothing compared to the white-hot fury she felt when she saw who one of the vampires was.

Angel.

He was standing there, his arms meekly at his sides, just like the vampires on either side of him. One was a tall Latino vampire, the other a short blonde. All three of them stood in front of Yaga, heads lowered. She was asking them questions, and they were answering.

Buffy had seen quite enough of that. Swallowing down the acidic bile in her throat, she stormed up to Yaga, repeating her question.

To make matters worse, Giles was just *standing* there sipping a cup of tea like nothing was happening.

"Excuse me, Slayer, but I am busy," Yaga said without looking at her. "Please continue your report," she said to the blonde.

"I searched the entire dockland area and found nothing, mistress."

Taking her stake out of her jacket pocket, Buffy then walked up to the blonde and plunged it into her chest.

As the blonde collapsed into dust, Yaga's eyes darkened. "How *dare* you?"

"How dare *I*? Who told you to turn Sunnydale's vampire population into your personal courier service?"

Stepping forward and getting right in Buffy's face,

Yaga said, "Have a care, Slayer. You are simply the latest in a line of short-lived girls, while I am immortal. I do not take kindly to—"

"I don't *care*." Buffy got right back in her face. "This is *my* operation, this is *my* town, this is *my* fight. You're here as a guest in *my* house. That means you don't get to pull this. *Especially* not with Angel."

"We have limited resources," Yaga said. "You are only one Slayer, whereas I can control an infinite number of vampires."

"No, actually, I'm two Slayers—and a swordsman, and a witch, and a Watcher, and plenty of other people. We don't need you going off the plan. Understand?"

"Are you threatening me, Slayer? What, exactly, do you intend to do?" Yaga asked with that sweet smile that made Buffy just want to punch her.

A pity she couldn't.

"Push me and you'll find out."

Yaga stared back at Buffy, who refused to back down.

For the second time, Yaga looked away. "Very well, Slayer. I will humor you for now."

Humor, my right toe. That's twice you've backed down, "Grandmother." Looks like you're not all that, bitch.

Buffy turned and staked the Latino vampire. As she did so, Angel blinked. "What—what happened?" He looked over at Yaga. "You."

Angel managed to cram an impressive amount of contempt into that one syllable.

Willow came into the library then. "Hey, everybody!

I got the root we needed from the magic shop."

"Excellent." Yaga smiled as if nothing was wrong. "All we need now is the Eye of Argon and we shall prepare. Ms. Rosenberg, you shall accompany me home, where we will retrieve the Eye."

Moving to stand between Yaga and Willow—who was looking a bit green all of a sudden—Buffy said, "What part of 'Willow's not going anywhere with you' didn't you get?"

"Try anything," Angel added in a quiet voice, "and you'll be next."

"Hardly." Yaga looked at Angel, and suddenly the vampire got down on all fours.

The bile rising in her throat once again, Buffy said, "Enough."

"Woof!" That was Angel, whose tongue was hanging out of his mouth.

Yaga turned her gaze on Buffy. "We have very little time, Slayer. I am willing to indulge you up to a point, but Koschei will be resurrected *very* soon. The Eye must be retrieved and I must school Ms. Rosenberg in its purpose."

"So why wait until the last minute if this eye is so important?"

"The Eye must remain frozen when it is not in use."

"Fine," Buffy said, "then use whatever defrosting spell you use and bring it back here, and *then* teach Willow."

"First of all," Yaga said, "there is no 'defrosting spell.' I will simply put it in the microwave."

"Oh," Buffy said in a small voice. Somehow she didn't picture a microwave in that house on chicken legs. Then again, she didn't picture a freezer, either. . . .

"Secondly, it will be more efficient if I teach her on the way."

Before Buffy could object again, Willow quickly said, "Buffy, it's okay. The ritual to revive Koschei is probably gonna be tonight. Time's a-wastin', y'know?" She tried to sound upbeat, but Buffy knew she was scared to death. To her credit, she wasn't letting that slow her down.

Sighing, Buffy said, "All right, go. But get back here *fast.*"

"Of course," Yaga said with that damn irritating smile, then she strode toward the exit. "Come, Ms. Rosenberg, there is still much to do."

After shooting Buffy an I'll-be-okay look—which was ruined a bit by the panic Buffy could see in her best friend's eyes—Willow said, "Coming!" and followed the sorceress out.

Turning to look at Giles, Buffy said, "And thank *you* for your support. Couldn't you have done something?"

"Perhaps I could have threatened her with an overdue fine," Giles said dryly, placing his teacup and saucer on the desk.

"That isn't funny, Giles."

In as quiet a tone as Buffy had ever heard Giles use, he said, "Neither is what she said when I first raised the objection to her using Angel in this way."

Buffy had known Giles for almost three years now,

and she knew that that tone wasn't a good one. Given the way Yaga had thrown the phrase "Avatar of Eyghon" around, Buffy suspected it had something to do with her ex-Watcher's misspent youth. That wasn't exactly Giles's comfort zone, and he didn't have Buffy's Slayerdom to back himself up with—for that matter, he didn't even have the Watchers anymore.

"Woof!"

Whirling around, she saw Angel was still on all fours, his tongue still hanging out of his mouth. He started rubbing the side of his head against Buffy's leg.

"She's a dead woman."

Chapter Twelve

Willow knew that Baba Yaga had a car, because she had been the one to turn up "Yulia Dryanushkinas"'s license, but for some reason she had been expecting it to be something other than a Ford Escort. It just seemed so . . . so *bland*.

But Willow didn't say anything out loud. She didn't want to take any chances on annoying someone who could turn her into a newt. Or a rat, like poor Amy.

Most of the drive was accomplished in silence, for which Willow was grateful. She was having trouble keeping all the spells straight in her head, especially since all of Baba Yaga's spells were in Russian. Willow had acquired a fairly decent grasp of Latin in the last year, which was what most of the spells she was familiar with were written in, and there was this one glamor in Etruscan that she was starting to get the hang of, but

Russian was just driving her batty. The vowels were funny, with all kinds of *y* sounds she wasn't expecting, and each word had more syllables than any language really should allow. It was as bad as that time she took German in eighth grade, only then it was hard consonants that had stumped her.

When they were almost at the split-level-that-wasn't, Baba Yaga suddenly spoke up. "You have shown tremendous aptitude, Willow—may I call you Willow?"

"Uh, sure, I guess."

"I haven't seen this level of potential for quite some time. If you were to ask, I would not refuse your petition to become my apprentice."

Willow shot the sorceress a look. "Petition? Uh, no—no petitions. I don't like petitions. People come up to you and they want you to sign their petition and they get all in your face and you usually just sign it to make them stop, and only later you find out you signed your name in support of animal testing for perfume and you feel terrible afterward. So no petitions for me, no way, no how."

Baba Yaga smiled, her full, perfect white teeth showing. "Very well, Willow. I hope you change your mind, but I will not try to convince you otherwise. As I told your Mr. Giles, I prefer my apprentices to be volunteers. It has been my experience that it is the only way to get a good one."

Those teeth—and the fact that a conversation had been started, so Willow didn't feel as silly asking a question now—prompted Willow to ask, "How come you don't appear like an old woman anymore? For that matter, why'd you even look like an old woman if you didn't have to?"

For several seconds, Baba Yaga said nothing. Then, as they turned onto Guterman Drive, she said, "There are two reasons. In Russia, in the 'old days,' as some would call them, with aging came respect. By appearing as an old woman, people—Russian people, people like Bulat—treated me with more deference than if I appeared the way I do now. In addition, it made me seem more fragile than I truly was—people assumed me to be infirm and physically weak. It served me well to be at once respected and underestimated."

Baba Yaga pulled the Escort into the municipal lot across from the house. Willow felt the ooglies in her protection spell, and tried not to shudder. "So why not appear like that now?"

"Preindustrial Russia and modern America are not the same. Here, the elderly are treated with disdain, nuisances to be discarded, and those who appear young and vital are far more likely to be taken seriously." She put the car into park and undid her seatbelt. "It is ridiculous to place greater value on callow youth than on experienced age, but it is one of many things about your country I find depressing." Opening the door, she said, "Come, let us retrieve the Eye."

Willow unbuckled her seat belt and got out as well, trying not to let it show how much the illusion spell was turning her stomach. She wished Baba Yaga would just take it down already. "What is the Eye of Argon, exactly?"

"Argon was a great sorcerer many thousands of years ago," Baba Yaga said as she started to walk across Guterman. "But he—"

She cut herself off, and also stopped walking. Her mouth was agape.

"What is it?" Willow asked, trying very, very, very hard not to panic.

"I smell a Russian."

That sent Willow into the very panic she didn't want, which manifested itself as a stomachache. It was as if a gnome had started running a bulldozer in her tummy. She'd read all the Russian fairy tales she could get her hands on, and that was what people like Baba Yaga and Koschei said when there was an intruder in their homes.

Baba Yaga raised her arms and started whispering the incantation to drop the illusion spell, which at once relieved and scared Willow. Her worst fear was that they were too late, that Koschei had already been res-urrected and was there to kill them both. That Willow would die without getting to say good-bye to Xander or Oz or Buffy—and worse, that Xander would already be dead, since Koschei was using seniors with rings to be resurrected, and the knowledge that Cordelia and Harmony were also dead did nothing to make her feel better.

But then the illusion dropped, and Willow again saw what she'd seen described in all the stuff she'd read: a giant hut resting on big chicken legs. Standing in front of the house was a sight that alleviated Wil-low's panic: Bulat. He was still wearing a tank top and shorts, looking very cut and toned, and holding his sword.

"What are you doing here, young Bulat?" Baba Yaga asked.

Bulat smiled. "I was waiting for you, Grandmother. I knew you had to return eventually for Eye of Argon."

"Did you find out where they took the seniors?" Willow asked.

"Oh, I know where they have been taken, Willow Rosenberg. I've known all along."

The gnome started the bulldozer back up. "What do you mean?"

Baba Yaga was shaking her head. "I should have known. You are in league with Koschei?"

"*Nyet,*" Bulat said, walking toward the two of them. "I am in league with your former apprentice, who will resurrect Koschei at long last."

"I don't get it," Willow said, the gnome having put the bulldozer into fifth gear. "You were the one who killed him!"

"To retrieve the love of my life, now long since dead. Times change, Willow Rosenberg, and now a great day is upon us, when Koschei the Deathless returns to the world. And you two will not be permitted to stop it."

"Oh—oh, yeah? Well, we'll just see about that," Willow said, trying to sound as much like Buffy as she could. "You show 'im," she said to Baba Yaga.

But Baba Yaga didn't move. Then Willow remembered what Buffy had said in the library the day Bulat first showed up—that the sorceress couldn't harm Bulat.

"She will show me nothing, okay?" Bulat grinned. He was now standing only a couple of feet in front of them, his sword raised high. "I have no wish to kill either of you. For one, even though she cannot harm me, I doubt that even this sword may kill the great Baba Yaga. And you, Willow Rosenberg, are an innocent pawn in this. But you will enter the hut of Baba Yaga and you will let me tie you up until after Koschei is resurrected."

"And after that?" Baba Yaga asked.

"After that it will not matter."

Willow debated the efficacy of turning and running away. If he wasn't big on killing, maybe he'd let her go.

No, if she ran away, she'd tell Buffy what had happened, and Bulat couldn't allow that. Just because he didn't *want* to kill her didn't mean he *wouldn't* kill her if he had to. And her running away would probably fall into the latter scenario. So Willow stayed put.

Bulat walked around behind Willow and Baba Yaga, sword pointing at their backs. "Okay, into the house."

"Do you really imagine this will work, young Bulat?" Baba Yaga asked as Bulat guided them toward the steps that led up into the hut. "Do you think you may imprison me in my own home?"

"Yes, I do, Grandmother. Because I know the secret of your house."

Willow followed Baba Yaga up the stairs. Inside

the door was a kitchen that looked just like a nineteenth-century kitchen she'd read about in this really cool book of Giles's. There was a large wrought-iron stove in the center, a storm sink with handles for faucets on one side, a big wooden chopping block, a wall full of knives and utensils, and a long counter, at one end of which was a dish rack. The only sops to modernity were tucked away in a corner: a giant refrigerator-freezer and next to it, mounted on the wall, a microwave. Willow assumed that the Eye of Argon was in the freezer and it would go in the microwave to defrost.

Assuming, of course, that Bulat the Brave let them proceed with their plan, which seemed pretty unlikely at the moment.

"Mrow!"

Looking down, Willow saw a small black cat pad into the kitchen. Instinctively, Willow got down on her knees and put out her hand for the cat to smell her. "Hi, kitty!" As the cat sniffed Willow's fingers, she looked up at Baba Yaga. "You didn't really strike me as a cat person."

In a tight voice Baba Yaga said, "I am not."

"You see," Bulat said, sounding annoyingly pleased with himself, "Grandmother here can control all things that are dead, and that includes everything in this house. All of it, you see, is dead—or was never alive. The only thing in this house that lives is Baba Yaga herself. The only way to wrest control of the house from her is to introduce a living creature that she has not allowed in—along with proper incantation."

Baba Yaga shook her head and stared at Bulat, her arms folded. "I assume Alfredo told you the incantation—as well as how to get past my defenses."

"Assume what you wish." Bulat shrugged and then said some words in Russian that Willow couldn't make out.

Then everything went dark.

Faith hadn't killed anything in hours. She was getting antsy.

She also hadn't found any sign of where Xander, Cordelia, and the rest of the students with class rings had gone. Faith had been surprised to learn that Xander had actually gone for that bogus ring crap. Xander was a good kid. Sure, she had expected him to have a little bit more experience, since he'd been sucking face with Cordelia, but the cheerleader was just like all the popular girls Faith knew back in Boston: lots of talk, but clueless when it came to the action.

However, Xander was a wicked fast learner and an eager student. Besides, he'd actually been in the game—longer than Faith, in fact—so he understood the postbattle rush.

And he let Faith stay on top while she showed him a new way to burn off that excess energy.

It didn't take Faith long to figure out that she wasn't the Slayer Xander *wanted* to be under. B, as usual, was totally oblivious, since she was all dreamy-eyed over Angel. Faith didn't get that. Sure, there was the whole true-love thing, but what did that have to do with sex? It was just a little fun, so why not take advantage of a stud who's already got the hots for you? It wasn't like it had to mean anything. Certainly *her* roll in the hay with Xander hadn't. (Of course, Faith was able to use Xander's frustration for her own benefit. . . .)

Shrugging and filing the thought away in the crowded compartment of her brain labeled "Stuff I Don't Get About Buffy," Faith continued her way along the railroad tracks. There were a ton of abandoned old structures alongside the tracks that went up and down the coast, and any one of them might have made a nice hidey-hole for this Alfredo guy. So far, though, all she'd found were a bunch of rats. Faith hated rats.

At least she had gotten rid of that damn cast over the weekend. Her wing was still a little tender, but she'd just lead with her left. . . .

Suddenly, as she left the shack she'd been searching, Faith heard something. The full moon was only a couple days ago, so she had some good moonlight, but she didn't see anything weird. Then she heard it again, and this time she was able to identify the sound: someone stepping on a twig.

Can't be a vamp—they don't stomp around like that. Figuring it was probably some dumb kid who literally was on the wrong side of the tracks, Faith moved slowly and cautiously toward the sound. She worked her way around the back of the shack, being careful not to touch anything or disturb the garbage on the grassy ground, just the way Professor Dormer and Sensei Kanno taught her before Kakistos—

Don't think about that.

Faith had to stop moving and get her breathing under control, as the malformed face of Kakistos suddenly formed in her vision, smiling at her like some kind of demonic clown, his one good eye glowering at her, his voice like a car driving on broken glass, saying her name oh-so-slowly, his fangs bared: *Faaaaaaiiiiiiiith.*

She forced the image out of her brain. *At least it's him with one eye.* Half the time when she dreamed of Kakistos she imagined him as how she had first seen him back in Boston, when he had both eyes. *Before I threw the axe, after—*

Don't think about that!

Another twig broke, bringing Faith back to the present. She worked her way to the corner of the shack, squatted down on her knees, and peered around the corner.

To her amazement, it *was* a vamp: a girl dressed in a bright flower-print summer dress of a type Faith wouldn't wear if you paid her. She was stumbling along toward the tracks in some kind of daze.

Then Faith remembered that that Yaga chick could control vampires. *Wonder if this is one of her minions? It's the only thing that explains her doing her "Night of the Living Undead" routine.*

Deciding not to bother with stealth, Faith walked toward the vamp. "Hey there, babe. Nice night for a stroll."

The vamp stopped, turned around, and stared at Faith for a second. She had her game face on, but her watery gray eyes looked all dead. "I have a message for the mistress."

Score one for the Southie Slayer. "You mean Baba Yaga? I can take the message."

"I must tell the mistress." The vamp turned around and started walking toward the tracks. "Koschei the Deathless will be resurrected in the DiFillippo Warehouse."

Faith frowned. She was still learning her way around town, but after growing up in Boston—where the streets were a tangle of paved-over horse paths—getting the Sunnydale map straight in her head was chicken feed. She was pretty sure the DiFillippo Warehouse was on the south side of town, and she was completely sure that that was where Bulat the Bulky was supposed to be checking things out.

"Thanks for the 411, bitch, but I got it from here."

The vamp, ignoring her, started across the tracks. She didn't see Faith remove the stake from her pocket and take aim. . . .

A second later, she was dust, and Faith was headed for the nearest pay phone. Bulat may have already called the info in, but Faith wanted to tell Giles herself, and it would be easier for her to go straight to the warehouse than detour to Slayer Central at the high school.

Digging into her pants pocket for a quarter while she ran toward one of the nearby buildings—a diner that was closed for renovations, but had a phone outside it—Faith considered Baba Yaga's ability to control the undead. *Y'know,* she found herself thinking, *when this is all over, we should ask Yaga to line up all the vamps in Sunnydale to take a stroll on the beach at sunrise. Then me and B can just party all night. . . .*

She arrived at the diner and pulled out a quarter from the pile of lint, keys, lipstick, and old T tokens she'd been carrying since she left Boston. Dropping everything else back into her pocket, she inserted the quarter and dialed the library.

"Mr. Giles speaking."

"Giles, it's Faith. I just found one of Baba Yaya's pet vamps. Said that the big shindig's happening at the DiFillippo Warehouse."

"It's Baba Yaga," Giles said, "and that's in Bulat's patrol zone."

Faith chuckled. Giles was cute when he got all correct-y, which was why she'd mispronounced the magic lady's name in the first place. "Whatever. Want me to head down there?"

"No, it's best if we go as a unit, and we're still awaiting Yaga and Willow's return. Come back to the library posthaste, and we'll map out a strategy." Giles sighed. "With Willow gone, I suppose I shall have to endeavor to locate the warehouse plans myself."

"Five by five, Giles. Be there in a flash." She hung up the phone, then turned and started jogging toward the main part of town. *Time to stop a resurrection and kick some ass.* Faith was unclear as to how much ass kicking would actually be involved—all she'd heard about was the big spell Willow was helping the Russian lady with—but Faith had been in Sunnydale long enough to know that ass kicking almost always wound up being part of the solution.

•   •   •

"Where *are* they?"

Buffy was pacing the library, sure she was about to wear a hole in the floor. Angel stood by the cage, having finally stopped barking like a dog and trying to hump Buffy's leg. When he had asked what happened, Buffy and Giles had exchanged a quick look and given no specifics, only that Yaga had whammied him. If it had been Xander who had been affected, Buffy likely would have provided explicit and heavily exaggerated details, but Xander also lived in a perpetual state of no dignity. Angel being in such a position was just wrong, and Buffy couldn't bring herself to actually *tell* him that he had been lying on the library floor grooming himself.

Giles was walking over to the main desk, saying, "I'll try calling."

That got Buffy to stop pacing. "She has a phone?"

"In addition to the microwave and the freezer, yes," Giles said with a grim smile. "She provided the number to me over the weekend." Picking up the phone, Giles punched the number in.

After about half a dozen eternities, Giles finally hung up. "No answer. And apparently her concessions to modernity do not include an answering machine."

"They should be here by now. It only takes five minutes to drive there and back, and it can't take more than another five to defrost the Eye of Calgon, or whatever it is. It's been half an hour."

"We're aware," Giles said quietly just as Faith came in, Oz and Michael right behind her.

"Found these two on the way, brought 'em back," the other Slayer said. "We good to go?"

"Not quite," Giles said. "It would seem that Baba Yaga and Willow have not returned. They might be in trouble."

"Let's get 'em out of trouble, then."

"It's not that simple," Giles said. "The counterspell can only work after the *Vozrozhdeniye* has commenced. If we can get to the warehouse before the ritual begins, a simple protection spell will neutralize the spell on the rings, and all will be well."

Michael raised his hand. "I can cast that."

"Excellent," Giles said. "If the *Vozrozhdeniye* has begun, however, we'll need to hold off Koschei until the counterspell can be cast."

"Angel and I can handle that," Buffy said.

Faith stepped forward. "You mean Angel, *Faith*, and I can handle that, B."

Buffy shook her head. "No, 'cause I need you to find Baba Yaga and Willow. Start at Yaga's place—it's at Guterman and Palombo."

Nodding, Faith said, "Yeah, okay."

"Any sign of tall, hot, and Russian?" Buffy asked Giles.

"No." Giles was digging into his pants pockets. "And I'm getting rather distressed about that." He pulled out a set of keys. "Faith, take my car, it'll be faster." He tossed the keys at Faith, who caught them with one hand.

"I'll try not to damage your ride too badly," she said with a grin.

Giles didn't say anything, but he didn't need to, as he had that Watcher Look of Suffering that Buffy had seen pretty much nonstop for almost three years. Longer than that, really—Merrick, her first Watcher, had had it too. Buffy figured Giles was reluctant to let Faith use his wheels, but, as Giles himself would say, *Needs must as the devil drives*. Literally, in this case.

Buffy looked at Oz. "We can take your van to the warehouse?"

"Sure," Oz said.

"Good." Turning to Faith, Buffy said, "You know how to get to Guterman and Palombo?"

Grinning, Faith said, "I learned how to drive in Massachusetts, B. I can find my way anywhere."

"Great. We don't have time to wait for Bulat—his sword would've been useful, but we'll deal. Let's go."

Chapter Thirteen

Buffy wasn't sure when it was, exactly, that she stopped being nervous before entering a situation in which there was every possibility she would be killed in a grisly fashion. Perhaps it was a byproduct of the one time she had entered such a situation and *was* killed in a grisly fashion, in a manner that allowed the Master to be freed from his prison beneath the city. Xander's knowledge of CPR had kept that from being permanent, but still, it was a nasty experience.

A part of her worried about the lack of nerves. On the one hand, she was good at what she did. After the nightmare of the Cruciamentum, Giles—who had very little reason to keep the Council's secrets after they canned him—explained several things about it. The thing that caught Buffy's attention was that many Slayers didn't undergo a Cruciamentum because they didn't live long enough to have one.

That had been an even bigger wakeup call than the Cruciamentum itself—which illustrated once and for all what creeps made up the Watchers' Council. Slayers weren't expected to live to adulthood. In fact, the Cruciamentum's purpose was in part to make sure a Slayer who lasted that long wasn't becoming too self-confident, too sure of herself.

Buffy supposed that that should have made her more humble, but it didn't. For one thing, despite the way the Watchers managed to *royally* screw up her Cruciamentum, she'd passed with flying colors. For another, the Watchers' wanting her to be more humble was, in her mind, the best reason not to be.

In any case, past success had led her to believe that she could handle herself, especially when she had so much help. Angel was by her side, and Faith, Willow, and Baba Yaga would be soon. And past failure reminded her that she should have stayed dead at the Master's hands—so every battle she was *able* to fight in was a victory, really, just because she showed up.

Oz's van pulled into the parking lot behind the DiFillippo Warehouse. If not for the dilapidated sign that said DIFILLIPPO in a lettering style that was all the rage in 1975, Buffy wouldn't have been able to tell it apart from the sixteen other warehouses in the area.

"They're definitely here," Oz said. He didn't elaborate, which suited Buffy fine. Giles got out on the passenger side, and Angel slid open the side door to allow him, Buffy, and Michael to exit the rear. The ex-Watcher had a sword that wasn't quite as impressive as

Bulat's, but Buffy knew that Giles could handle it quite well. Oz had a crossbow, and Michael had a few of the icky things you needed to cast spells.

Looking up at the roof, Oz said, "Seems quiet."

Giles unfolded the printout he'd made. The one advantage to having waited so long for Willow and Yaga to not show up was that Giles had used the time to tame the computer and get it to provide him with the layout of the warehouse. "According to this," he said, "there is a rear door, a front door, and a large delivery entrance."

Buffy looked over at the warehouse. She could see the delivery entrance, which was boarded up. She was willing to bet the doors were as well.

Then she looked up and saw a light shining out from the middle of the roof. "Giles, is there a sky-light?"

Peering down, Giles said, "Er—yes, there is."

Indicating the light with her head, Buffy said, "I'm thinking that the lights are on, and somebody's home." She looked down a bit at the wall. There was a window about twenty feet up. *I should be able to jump that.* "I'm gonna go to the roof, do some recon through the skylight."

Both Giles and Angel said "Buffy, be careful" at the same time, which would've made Buffy laugh under different circumstances, but she didn't wait to see the look on either of their faces as she jogged back a bit and then made a run for the warehouse. Her sneaker soles collided with the driveway pavement, building up speed, and then she jumped, her enhanced muscles taking her a lot higher than a typical five-foot-two eighteen-year-old would be able to leap. *Can't quite do tall buildings in a single bound,* she thought as she reached out and grabbed the windowsill, *but it'll do.*

Thrusting her feet out, she was able to slam her soles into the side of the warehouse, thus keeping her knees from doing it, which would've hurt. She hung there for a second, fingers trying to solidify their grip on the windowsill, feet flush against the wall, and took a breath. Then another. And then she kicked out with her feet, pivoted with her hands and wrists, and flipped backward and up onto the roof.

She landed, wincing and crying "Whoulf!" as she felt something twist in her back. *Still not back to full Slayer strength, dammit. Gotta watch that.* Yet another one she could thank the Sisterhood of Jhe for . . .

Gingerly, she made her way over to the skylight, one of three on the roof, but the only one light was coming from. She peered down, and tried not to gasp.

An area had been cleared of boxes, and the displaced boxes almost made a wall around where the ritual was taking place. There was a circle drawn in chalk on the floor. In the center of the circle stood someone with a bald head and a hook nose. She couldn't see his face all that clearly but surmised that this was probably Alfredo, Yaga's former apprentice and the dispenser of Avanas'ev school rings. He was wearing a brown robe of a type people who did these rituals *always* wore, and right in front of him was a human body. She couldn't make out the body's features, as it was surrounded by a purple mist.

Buffy had a bad feeling that the body inside the mist used to be Peter Burton and was about to be Koschei. Especially since little strings of magical energy were flying out of the mist and attaching to the people standing on the circumference (*Thank you, Mr. Hanbridge, for the Geometry Class of Doom*) of the circle. Buffy didn't recognize everyone in that circle from her vantage point, but she quickly caught sight of Xander, Cordelia, Harmony, Jonathan, Larry, the non-Oz members of Dingoes Ate My Baby, and a few others.

Every instinct in Buffy's body screamed *Jump through the skylight and kick ass,* but that might have wound up hurting her friends and classmates more than helping them. *Better check in with Giles first, and form an* actual *plan. Besides, not much point in bringing Angel, Giles, and Oz along just to have them stand outside while I do all the work.*

Jogging over to the edge of the roof, she peered over the side, made sure the ground was clear, and then leapt off the ledge. A moment of freefall, and then she hit the pavement, bending her knees to absorb as much of the impact as possible. Still, pain shot through her calves and knees, and she fell almost into a full squat before recovering.

She rose to see the other four standing by, concerned looks on their faces. "This is the place, all right." She gave a quick description of what she had seen.

Giles shook his head. "Damn. The *Vozrozhdeniye* has already commenced." He looked at Michael. "I'm afraid the protection spell won't do us much good at this point."

"I can still cast it on you guys. Every little bit helps, right?"

"It won't work on me," Angel said, "but you should cast it on the others."

Michael frowned. "Why not?"

Buffy shot Angel a look. They hadn't explained about Angel to Michael. "Uh . . . ," Angel began.

Then Buffy just went ahead and said it: "Angel's a vampire. But he's a good one—it's a long story."

"Uhhh—okay." It didn't sound okay, but Michael didn't say anything else, just sat down on the pavement in what Buffy knew from Willow was the lotus position. A few minutes later, she felt all tingly.

Michael got to his feet. "All done. Not sure what good it'll do, though."

Giles put a hand on Michael's shoulder and gave him a smile, which surprised Buffy, as that wasn't Giles's usual style. "As you said, every little bit helps." Removing his hand, Giles turned around and looked out toward the road. "I hope Faith arrives soon."

"What can we do in the meantime that won't get all the seniors killed?" Buffy asked.

"It takes approximately twenty minutes after the resurrection for it to become permanent, after which point even the counterspell won't work. It's a short window, but it's all we have."

"Can we do anything to Alfredo?"

Giles shook his head. "The circle probably protects him."

Angel finally spoke. "From the living, maybe, but this is necromancy—I'm dead, so I might be immune."

Giles got that frowny face he got when someone thought of something he hadn't. "I'm afraid my knowledge of the subject is limited."

"Worth a try, though," Buffy said. "Oz, you and Michael stay here and keep an eye out for Faith."

Oz nodded, hefting his crossbow. "Will do." Michael just nodded.

"Giles and I'll go in the back way. Angel, think you can get up there?" She pointed at the roof.

"Sure."

"Good—you do the dramatic-entrance-through-the-skylight thing."

He smirked. "Always was a fan of the classics."

"Let's do it."

Buffy started moving around to the other side of the warehouse, Giles right behind her, sword out. He whispered, "It's a good plan, Buffy."

"I just hope we can hold the dead deathless guy off long enough."

"Indeed."

They came to the back entrance, which was boarded up, just like the other one. However, this one had a bunch of two-by-fours nailed across the doorway, instead of one big board. Buffy walked up to the door and grabbed the one in the center and yanked on it. The nails ripped out of the doorframe with a satisfying crunching noise of twisting metal, only to reveal a padlock on the door itself. Sighing, Buffy turned so she was perpendicular (*Thanks again, Mr. Hanbridge*) to the doorway, picked up her left leg, bent slightly to her right, and then let loose with a side kick to the padlock. The wooden door caved in a bit near where the lock was attached, but it didn't break, so she hit it with another side kick, then a third.

Finally, it splintered, and the door swung open. Grateful that it opened inward, Buffy then yanked off two more two-by-fours, which provided enough room for Buffy and Giles to enter the building.

Still whispering as they climbed between the slats, Giles said, "It's likely that Mr. LaManna will have some manner of sentry. We should be on the looko— *oof!*"

Buffy whirled around just in time to see Giles collapse to the floor, having been hit on the head by Bulat the Brave.

"Such a pity," he said. "I was truly hoping, you see, that you would not find the location of the *Vozrozhdeniye* until after the ceremony was complete. This is why I—what is the word?—volunteered to 'search' this portion of your town."

"And you were telling us *Yaga* couldn't be trusted?" Buffy asked, suddenly very pissed off—at herself as much as anything.

"I did not lie, Buffy Summers. Baba Yaga may not be trusted."

"Neither, apparently, may you." Buffy bent over and picked up Giles's sword. "But if you think you're gonna stop me—"

Bulat stepped over Giles, his sword raised. "I do not need to stop you, Slayer of Vampires, I need only to delay you." He held the sword up in the *en garde* position.

Buffy hesitated for a second, then turned on her heels and ran.

Just as Faith and Buffy had been caught offguard by Katherine Toomajian pulling that trick, it took Bulat a few seconds to get his mind around the notion of his opponent turning tail and running. Buffy remembered what Giles had said about Bulat's fighter's ethic, so he probably never expected a "true warrior" like her to rabbit.

But it gave her a head start, and that was all that mattered in her world.

The warehouse was a maze of boxes and crates piled on top of each other. She ran randomly through them, not picking any particular direction, figuring it would make it easier to lose Bulat.

At one point, she saw a box on top of a crate that looked like it was teetering on the brink of falling down onto the passageway next to it. Buffy decided to turn into the small corridor. But the first thing she saw when she turned the corner was Bulat, running toward her. *Well, that plan blew.*

"A valiant effort, Slayer," Bulat said as he ran toward her, "but chase is ended, okay?"

Glancing at the teetering box, Buffy picked up her right leg, bent to her left, kicked, and then ran like hell. She had no idea what was in that box, but it was about to land on Bulat's head.

Dashing between the crates, she hoped that a blow to the head would hold him off long enough. She needed to stop wasting time with this cat-and-mouse stuff and stop Koschei from being resurrected.

• • •

Angel knelt at the skylight, peering down into it, watching as dozens of young people had their life drained to resurrect Koschei, and he waited for some sign from Buffy or Giles. Better a two-front attack, after all.

One thing was for sure: They couldn't risk Koschei's resurrection. Angel had first heard of the sorcerer from the Master. It was one of the rare times that Angelus actually was willing to be in the old vampire's presence, and—as usual—it was only because of Darla. She had been devoted to the Master, and Angelus had been devoted to her, and so when the Master called, she always answered. Sometimes, Angelus was willing to go with her. *And sometimes I just stayed home and told her to bugger off,* he thought with a grim smile. *Like the night Drusilla brought young William Pratt home.* That sad poet had been made by Drusilla into a vampire named Spike. When Darla returned, the four of them cut a swath through Europe and Asia—at least until the massacre of a Romany tribe changed Angel's life forever . . .

Shaking his head, he pushed those memories down with the other bad ones. Of course, that mental compartment was massive and full to bursting by now, particularly after his sojourn through hell. Angel had spent the last century learning how to keep the evil that he'd seen and that he'd done (mostly that he'd done) from overwhelming him.

Right now, he needed to focus on Koschei. The Master and Koschei had clashed back in the day, and the Master had lost. The ancient vampire had survived only by the skin of his malformed teeth, but no method of killing Koschei worked. In fact, it was in part his encounter with Koschei that led the Master to study the magic arts.

Every time we think it ends, it begins again, he thought.

Now someone was trying to resurrect Koschei, just as Absalom and the Anointed One had tried to bring the Master back. Buffy had stopped it then, and she'd stop it now—again, with Angel's help.

And how long do you think you can do this?

It would have been so much easier, he knew, if he hadn't fallen in love. He could have just played the mysterious informant, tried to bring the balance back, like Whistler had told him he was destined to do, and aided Buffy in her fight against the forces of darkness. But they had fallen in love—almost instantly, truth be told—and nothing was ever the same. The curse the Romany had put upon him had an "out" clause, and the night he and Buffy consummated their love had triggered it. He did not deserve to be happy, as far as they were concerned, so happiness brought about its own punishment: reverting to Angelus, the monster he had been.

Eventually, Buffy had been forced to send him to hell—killing him, really, although like Buffy herself, and perhaps soon like Koschei, he had come back. Again, he fought by her side, whether against a rogue Watcher or the Sisterhood of Jhe or Spike during his less-than-triumphant return to Sunnydale. But he couldn't afford to fall in love with her again.

That's stupid. You are in love with her, and she with you. And it's only a matter of time before you both have to address that.

Again, Angel shoved the unpleasant thoughts away. There was still no sign of Buffy or Giles, and it looked like Koschei was starting to come alive—the corpse on the floor had started to twitch.

I've gotta move. He stood upright and leapt in the air, his booted feet crashing into the skylight. The shards of broken glass that sliced at his face and hands didn't bother him—when one healed as fast as a vampire did, cuts and scrapes were all but meaningless— they only added to the effect of his entrance.

The necromancer looked up at Angel, and then smiled even as he continued the chanting he'd been doing all along. Angel didn't like the look of that.

He liked it even less when he suddenly halted in midair, right above the ritual. The glass continued to fall, some of it on the students, who were as oblivious to their cuts and scrapes as Angel, but for a different reason.

Angel couldn't move. He couldn't even blink. His guess that, as an undead creature, he could penetrate a necromancer's circle was apparently a wrong one. Now he was trapped like a fly in amber, forced to hover helplessly while a hundred Sunnydale High School students, including Xander and Cordelia, died.

He couldn't even scream in frustration.

This was not the plan. . . .

Chapter Fourteen

I have got to start a pool to help get Giles a new ride, was Faith's first thought upon encountering the librarian's wheels. He drove a Citroen, which Faith associated with the old biddies in Back Bay, not cool dudes like Giles. Hell, a Citroen was the kind of car Professor Dormer would—

Don't think about that.

Slamming the cranky old car into gear—a feat that actually required a certain amount of Slayer strength—Faith pulled out of the Sunnydale High faculty parking lot and headed toward Guterman Drive.

When she turned onto the street, she nearly crashed the Citroën onto the sidewalk at what she saw. It took her a moment to wrench the steering wheel straight and get the car back on track. Faith took several deep breaths as she pulled into the municipal lot, not bothering to pay attention to the lines.

It was one thing to be told you were going to a fairy-tale house on chicken legs, but a whole other thing to actually see it. That was as freaky a sight as Faith had ever seen, and this after growing up in South Boston and spending most of the past year as a Slayer.

In Faith's defense, she hadn't expected to see the house in its current state. Yaga was supposed to be keeping that illusion spell on it, making it look all nice and suburban. *So if the illusion's down, that probably means something happened to the lady casting the illusion.*

Closing the car door, but not bothering to lock it on the theory that no self-respecting car thief would get anywhere near Giles's junk heap, Faith dashed across Guterman and approached the house. It was surrounded by a fence made out of bones, with six posts topped off with skulls. Faith kinda liked this Bizarro-world version of the white picket fence. Since she knew damn well that she was never going to get near the ideal world that a traditional fence represented—neither as a Southie juvenile delinquent nor as a Slayer—she liked the twisted imagery.

I don't remember B saying anything about a fence, Faith thought as she reached out to open the gate.

Then she stopped, because if Buffy hadn't mentioned it . . .

She didn't even get the chance to finish the thought, since the bones of the fence started to rattle and hum. *Probably too much to hope that they'll turn into U2 on me,* Faith thought as she stepped back into the defensive position that Sensei Kanno had taught her back in Boston before—

Dammit, don't think *about that!*

The bones of the fence started to come apart and swirl in the air, making a noise like twelve people typing really fast. It looked like a tornado of remains stood between Faith and the hut.

After a minute, the swirling slowed down, and the bones came together into a skeleton that was about nine feet tall. Instead of hands, the skeleton had two of the skulls at the end of each arm, another two skulls embedded in the chest, and two on top of the body instead of the usual one.

All six skulls started to laugh. At least, Faith guessed they were laughing—the jaw bones were moving up and down, the teeth banging into each other, so they all made a frantic clicking noise, like crickets on steroids.

The skeleton just stood there. *Probably waiting for me to make the first move.*

Faith had always been pretty low on virtues, and patience wasn't one of the few she had. Besides, there was a clock—that voz-roz-hootenany or whatever it was could be going on right now, and they needed Yaga and Willow to stop it.

So it was time for her to smack down Skeletor.

She tried running around the skeleton, but he just took one big step to the side to block Faith's way. Then she broke left, but he just stepped in her way again.

Without breaking stride, she faked right, went left again, and then jumped in the air. *Sensei always said I had a mean jumping side kick,* she thought as the blade of her foot collided with one of the skulls in her opponent's chest.

It was like kicking a brick wall—something Faith had actually done once or twice. Skeletor didn't even budge, and she fell to the ground in a heap, grateful she had worn shoes with heels, which lessened the impact on her feet.

Clambering backward, she saw that the skeleton wasn't following her. He just wasn't going to let her into the house.

She ran toward him again, this time being sure to kick low, in the thing's legs.

Skeletor stumbled this time, but didn't budge beyond that. *Dammit.*

Every time she backed off, Skeletor didn't move. It was like there was an invisible line, and he wouldn't move as long as Faith didn't cross it.

Unfortunately, Faith had to cross it if she was going to check out the house. She didn't know for sure if Willow and the crazy lady were in there, but a guard dog usually meant there was something worth guarding. *Or it's just Yaga's usual security system.*

But Faith couldn't afford to presume that, and besides, Skeletor was starting to seriously piss her off, and she wasn't about to let herself get beat by a pile of bones. So she ran straight at him. Punching him would be a *bad* idea. Her right arm wasn't at full strength, and she wasn't sure she'd be able to do much against solid bone but bruise her knuckles. So she planned to go at Skeletor with a side kick, followed by a spinning hook kick, then an axe kick, before finally leaning in with a left hook.

She got about halfway through that, but in the middle of the spin kick, Faith felt something jar against her ankle. Skeletor had whacked her in the leg with the skull at the end of his arm, and Faith went sprawling. She tried to convert her fall into a roll, but her right arm collapsed, sending pain shooting through her entire right side as she ate dirt. Bracing herself with her left arm, she kicked up at Skeletor, catching him in the leg just as he was about to swing down onto Faith's back. Her kick deflected him, but she wasn't about to give him another shot. She scrabbled back across the dirt toward the street.

Naturally, Skeletor stopped moving and went back to his "at ease" position.

This isn't working. Faith knew if she stayed at it long enough, she'd figure out a way to get through the Bad-ass of Bones, but she didn't have that kind of time.

Then she remembered that when she and B had gone up against Kakistos, and an ordinary stake hadn't done the trick. Kakistos had smiled and said, "I guess you'll need a bigger stake"—the one thing that monster ever said that was worth listening to, since she had then taken a hunk of wood the size of Cleveland and rammed it into his chest, dusting the bastard who'd killed her Watcher. *The question is, what can I—?*

Then she grinned. Scrambling to her feet, she ran back to the parking lot. Folding herself into Giles's car, she turned the key and gunned it—or at least tried to.

I'm definitely taking up a collection, she thought as she accelerated the Citroën out of the municipal lot and toward the hut on chicken legs.

By the time she got it across Guterman, the Citroën had accelerated all the way to twenty, and Faith—who hadn't bothered with a seat belt—went flying when the car hiccupped onto the sidewalk, her hair brushing against the top of the car. Her buttocks got sore from the landing, and she decided that, if she couldn't swing a new car for Giles, she'd at least get him a decent suspension.

The speedometer needle was moving past thirty when she drove up onto the dirt and rocks making a beeline for Skeletor, who still wasn't moving, since the car hadn't crossed the line.

Then the Citroën slammed hard into Skeletor, jerking Faith forward, right into the steering wheel. Hot pain knifed through her chest as she hit the brakes. Her ribs had pretty much healed, but banging into the wheel wasn't doing them any favors. *Airbags, to go with the suspension.*

The car skidded along the dirt, bones flying everywhere, the car whirling around. Suddenly, Faith was jarred to the right, as the driver's side of the car slammed into the house. Luckily, it was off the ground, so the bottom of the house only hit the top of the low-slung Citroën. It blocked the driver's side door, though, so Faith clambered across to the passenger side, trying to ignore the aching in her chest, and got out.

The ground was covered in bones and skulls.

Luckily, they didn't move. *Some Russian wizard wasn't expecting a demolition derby.*

She jogged over to the front door of the house, leaving the Citroën behind and not giving it a second thought. The door was closed, and the handle was too high off the ground for Faith to reach. However, the floor stuck out just enough under the bottom of the door for her to get a toehold. Backing up a few feet, she ran and jumped up. Reaching out, she was able to snag the door handle with her right hand—which was good, 'cause the toehold on the floor wasn't offering any traction. The handle was one of those pull-down types instead of a knob, so Faith just let her weight pull it down, then she let go and dropped to the ground.

Bending her knees as she landed, she looked up to see the door slowly open inward. Once again she backed up and did a running jump, this time landing inside the house.

The room she was in was dark, and it looked like an old-fashioned kitchen, like the stuff in the old colonial museums in Boston. Well, except for the fridge and microwave.

"Willow? You here?"

N hing.

Slowly, she moved farther into the room. It was pretty unlikely that Skeletor was the only defense.

"Willow?"

"Mrow?"

Faith looked down to see a black cat standing in the doorway to whatever the next room was. *Figures, the crazy old lady is a crazy old cat lady.* Ignoring the feline, she walked into the next room.

It was a living room, with paintings of forests on the walls; old, worn-out furniture, including a couch, a love seat, and a big chair; and a small wooden writing desk off to the side. Faith barely noticed the décor, however, because the dominant features of the room were the two bodies hanging in midair: Yaga and Willow, both fast asleep.

Well, now I know why they didn't answer. And why they haven't shown up to cast the counterspell.

"Mrow!"

Faith turned to see the cat standing in the doorway. "Go 'way, moggie," she said, turning her back on the cat. She had bigger problems—like how to get Willow and Yaga down.

Screw it, the direct approach worked last time. She reached up and grabbed Willow's arm, which sent a massive jolt of electricity searing through her hand. Faith tried to let go, but couldn't. Her whole body felt like it was on fire, and she tried to let go, but couldn't, and it hurt so much. . . .

Then, suddenly, it stopped. Faith fell to the floor, feeling like she'd just run a marathon. A high-pitched squealing sound came from the area of the ceiling, and she looked up to see that Willow and Yaga weren't there anymore. They'd been replaced with some kind of bat-winged creature that looked like a pterodactyl on a meth bender. It had a huge mouth full of teeth that was wide open and squealing as it started to fly around the room, buzzing Faith's head.

The Slayer just grinned. *Something I can hit.* Getting to her feet, she tried to punch the thing as it flew by, but it dodged her each time.

"Faith, you're wasting your time."

"Oof!" Faith cried, as the monster slammed into her, knocking the wind out of her and sending her flying into the love seat. The voice had sounded like Yaga's, and it was in her head. *What the hell?*

"I cannot maintain this link for long—I've only been able to do this much with Willow's help. The Forbrat demon is just a distraction. You must destroy the cat."

"No!" Willow's voice now sounded in Faith's head. *"It's just an innocent kitty!"*

"It is no such thing—it merely has the appearance of a feline to distract the unwary into—"

"Hey, any chance you two could bitch at each other somewhere outta my head?" Faith asked as she dove to the floor to avoid another sweep from the Forbrat, which kept ducking her own punches.

"Kill the cat, and then we will be . . ."

The voice disappeared. *Great.* Faith ducked the Forbrat again and pulled out her stake. She wasn't too keen on the idea of just killing an innocent cat, but if that would set Willow and Yaga free, it was worth it.

The Forbrat was smart, though—it swooped down and got in Faith's way. Luckily, it came close enough that Faith was able to sock it in the face with a good left hook, one that she threw all her strength behind.

Her knuckles were sore, but the punch sent the demon flying into the wall, splitting one of the paintings in two. *Never was much for art anyhow,* Faith thought with a grin as she leapt on top of the Forbrat demon and hit the sucker over and over again in the face for about ten seconds.

"Mrow?"

Looking up from the demon, Faith saw that the cat was now on approach. She had dropped her stake on the floor and now crawled over to get it.

Then she hesitated. If someone had pointed at a vamp or a demon or even a person and told her, "Kill that and everything'll be fine," she wouldn't have had a problem. But a cat? It was just an innocent creature.

Screw it, she thought, *the world's fulla victims.* She rammed the stake down into the top of the cat's head. Blood spurted out as the stake cut through fur and flesh.

"Mreeeeeeoooooowwwwww!" The cat cried out in agony that tugged at emotions Faith pretended she didn't have, even as the animal started to glow.

Shielding her eyes as it glowed brighter, Faith backed off quickly, since glowing magic things almost never meant anything good. Sure enough, it glowed almost as bright as the sun for just a second.

Faith blinked the spots out of her eyes after it dimmed, and looked around to watch as the Forbrat demon fell to the ground, and she saw that the cat wasn't a cat anymore, but some other kind of demon. The only thing that was the same was the stake through its head.

Willow and Yaga were now standing in the room. The Russian lady was already moving toward the kitchen. "We must hurry."

"You're welcome, bitch!" Faith called out after her. Then she shook her head and winced.

Willow walked up to her. "You okay?"

"Five by five." Then she smiled. "Okay, maybe five by four. But I'll live."

"I'm just glad that wasn't really a cat."

"Gotta do what you gotta do," Faith said with a shrug. "Crazy lady's right, though, time's a-wastin'. We gotta get to the warehouse."

"What warehouse?"

Faith started walking toward the kitchen, figuring Willow would follow. "The DiFillippo Warehouse. I found one of Yaga's vamps, and she let loose with the info. B and the gang are there now, trying to hold off Mr. Deathless until we get there."

"I know that place!" Willow said. "It's on the south side, right where Bulat was supposed to be looking for the seniors. Figures."

"Whaddaya mean?"

As Faith came into the kitchen, Yaga was putting something in the microwave. "She means that young Bulat is working with Alfredo to resurrect Koschei. It was he who turned my home against me, with the help of the Forbrat demon, and imprisoned us."

Faith blinked. "Bulat the Bulky was workin' for the bad guys? Didn't think he had the stones. I'm impressed."

"I am disgusted," Yaga said as she closed the microwave door, pressed some keys, and then hit START, "but not especially surprised. Young Bulat has always been a fool."

"Damn." Faith shook her head. "If he went to the warehouse after screwing with you guys, B and the others might be walkin' feetfirst into trap-land. We gotta motor."

The microwave beeped. Yaga opened the door and took out what was inside—which Faith saw was a giant, bloodshot blue eye inside a bell jar. This reminded Faith of two things: why she hated magic, and what she'd had for lunch, 'cause it was rising up from her stomach to the bottom of her throat. "You really need that?"

"We really do. And as I said, we must hurry."

Jerking her thumb toward the front door, Faith said, "I've got Giles's car, but I'm not sure it's in perfect working order."

Willow's eyes went a lot wider than saucers. "Giles *let* you use his car?"

Shrugging, Faith said, "It was his idea."

"Wow—he really *is* mellowing without the Watchers."

"A car is not sufficiently swift for the purpose," Yaga said. Then she gave that annoying smile again. "Luckily, I have something better."

Chapter Fifteen

It had been a very long time since Bulat the Brave had been this frustrated.

He was on the cusp of finally ending it all, of achieving the freedom that he'd desired for so very long, and this tiresome little girl was making things difficult for him.

At first, of course, immortality had been just wonderful. The inability to die had obvious advantages, but it hadn't occurred to him until the first time he was wounded—while sparring with Ivan—that it also meant he was unable to get hurt. It made battle so much more entertaining, and so much easier, for he could eschew defensive tactics and focus on a purely offensive strategy. Already a brilliant fighter, he became the finest warrior in Russia.

And then Ivan died, poisoned during an attempted

rebellion. Bulat had managed to put the rebellion down, but not until after his best friend was killed. Luckily, by then Prince Aleksandr, the heir to the throne, to whom Vasilisa had given birth two decades prior, was ready to take over. King Aleksandr made Bulat the official protector of his kingdom, and gave him Vasilisa for his bride.

(Aleksandr never knew that all he was doing was reuniting his true parents. Ivan had never been able to bring himself to overcome his revulsion for Vasilisa's physical form, so one night when Bulat and Ivan shared a bed—which happened rather often—the king asked his dearest friend to sleep with Vasilisa so the kingdom could have an heir. This had been an easy favor for Bulat to grant, of course, since his nights not spent in Ivan's bed were already spent in Vasilisa's—they simply no longer needed to be circumspect about it.)

It wasn't until Bulat noticed that Vasilisa was turning rather old and ugly that he started to see the downside to immortality.

Worse, Vasilisa started becoming unstable, forgetting who Bulat and Aleksandr were, not remembering Ivan, not even remembering who she was. Eventually, Bulat could not bear to watch the love of his life become wrinkly and disgusting while he remained young and vital, so he left his wife and unknowing child behind and traveled the world.

Centuries passed, and Bulat was truly frustrated. The world changed, but he had no interest in changing with it. He missed the forests of Russia, and the ability to live by nothing but the power of his charm and skill with the sword. He had many lovers, men and women alike, but none could live up to the ideal of his dearest friend and his lady love. Without Ivan or Vasilisa, his life was purposeless.

He had even gone back to Baba Yaga, begging her to make him mortal again, but she just laughed at him, saying that only Koschei's resurrection could bring that about.

Many times he had tried to kill himself. Every time, he failed. By the end of the twentieth century, he had attempted every imaginable method of suicide, and many that were unimaginable. There was always a war being fought somewhere, and Bulat had enlisted in hundreds of armies in the hopes that the devastating weaponry of the modern age would do what blades and muskets could not, but even there he was denied.

And then he met Alfredo LaManna.

Now he had a way to finally die the death for which he'd yearned so long. All he had to do was delay the Slayer until Alfredo completed the ritual.

She had led him on a merry chase, young Buffy Summers had. Of course, she had help—Bulat had known several Slayers in his time, but he had never known one to have such an extensive support network, not to mention a second Slayer to call upon—and that had proven frustrating. But, ultimately, it had been for naught. After all, he was Bulat the Brave, and no matter how much she forced him to chase her through this warehouse, no eighteen-year-old girl would be anything more than a minor nuisance.

At least, that was what he thought right up until someone kicked him in the small of his back. While his wounds healed almost instantly, he still felt pain, and the blow struck several nerves that made Bulat's legs go numb and his knees buckle under him, sending him to the floor. He lost his grip on his sword, and it slid across the warehouse floor with a metallic scrape that made Bulat wince. It came to rest with the blade sticking out from under a crate a few feet away.

"Gotcha," Buffy said, then kicked him in the ribs for good measure.

But he was Bulat the Brave, the finest warrior in all Russia, and he would not be defeated this way. He lashed out and grabbed Buffy's ankle, yanking it toward him and causing her to fall on the floor as well. He then reached out and grabbed the hilt of his sword and pulled, but it would not give. Suddenly, pain shot through his hand as Buffy—who had somehow managed to get up in a matter of seconds—stepped on his hand.

"Ah, ah, ah—don't touch that sword."

With her other foot, she kicked him in the face.

Bulat didn't let it bother him. He was indestructible until Alfredo finished the *Vozrozhdeniye*—and after that, he wouldn't care. As she reared back to kick him again, he grabbed her ankle a second time, again throwing her to the floor.

He got to his feet, bent over, and pulled harder on the sword, this time freeing it.

Turning around, he saw Buffy had again leapt to her feet. *She is agile,* he thought, then remembered that this *wasn't* just a girl, this was the Slayer. While she appeared to be even more fragile than Vasilisa was when Bulat finally left Russia, in truth she was, if not Bulat's equal, as close as any mortal could be.

Now Bulat was standing between Buffy and anywhere she could go, as her back was to the crates. She couldn't turn and take the coward's path now. Bulat held his sword aloft. He was tired of this girl fighting him on her terms—which meant using her agility and speed to be the mouse to Bulat's cat. It was time to change the terms to something that was more advantageous to Bulat. Even if she *were* the finest swordswoman in this or any land, she was only eighteen. Bulat's had become the finest sword arm in Russia when he was only a few years older than Buffy, and he'd had centuries since to hone his craft.

She would be no match for him.

Buffy held up her sword as well, and did so, Bulat noticed, properly. She was indeed trained. "You wanna do the Errol Flynn thing, that's fine with me."

"Excellent. It has been too long since I have been challenged."

"I'd say you've been mentally challenged all along," she said, and then swung her sword, aiming for the most obvious strike imaginable.

As he parried with ease, Bulat thought, *Perhaps not that well trained.* Buffy followed with another overhead swing, which he also easily parried.

But then stars went in front of his eyes as Buffy's foot collided with his genitals, and he bent over, unable to breathe. Yet Bulat somehow managed to lift his arm to parry when Buffy swung around to try to finish him off.

Forcing himself past the pain, Bulat continued to parry Buffy's strikes, all the while resolving never to underestimate her again. She wasn't overwhelmingly skilled, but she knew she was the inferior warrior, and so compensated.

The pain in his groin started to subside. Bulat had had many children over the centuries, though he'd long since lost track of them, and so wasn't concerned for his future ability to procreate. Besides, if all went well, he'd be dead within the next half-hour or so.

Buffy kept pushing him back and Bulat kept letting her, taking Buffy's measure. She was indeed well trained; Bulat recognized her style of fighting as a fairly classic British fencing style. Having met her Watcher—and given that it was his sword she was brandishing—this wasn't much of a surprise. He could smell the spices and hear the chanting of Alfredo now, which meant they were near the end of the *Vozrozhdeniye*.

Suddenly, Buffy's eyes went wide, her attention drawn to something behind Bulat. "Angel!"

Seeing his advantage, Bulat pressed, finally going on the offensive. Buffy was able to parry, but now Bulat had her wholly on the defensive. Bulat was pleased to hear the clang of metal on metal as their swords struck, and he could feel the vibration in Buffy's sword. She was strong, yes, but so was he, and it was getting to her.

Out of the corner of his eye, he caught sight of the

ritual, and saw that the corpse he'd stolen from the morgue was floating about a foot off the floor and was twitching. The surrounding students were starting to look rather pale.

It will all be over soon.

Then Buffy did something Bulat hadn't expected: She leapt over him, flipping over his head and landing behind his back. Before he could react, he felt the cold steel of her blade slice into his back.

Once, such things would have concerned him, but Bulat had long since grown accustomed to the pain of being impaled, and so it was nothing for him to turn around and swing his sword at the Slayer.

But she had already turned and run toward where Alfredo was performing the *Vozrozhdeniye,* having left the sword in Bulat's back.

"You should have stabbed me in the leg, okay?" Bulat said with a sneer as he ran to catch up to her.

But she reached the circle before he did. Not that it mattered, as she couldn't get through the wards, and ended up slamming into them headlong, which sent her sprawling.

To Bulat's horror, it also sent Alfredo sprawling, his incantation interrupted as he cried out in pain and clutched the sides of his head. When that happened, the corpse that would house Koschei's essence fell to the floor with a meaty thud.

Buffy had a huge smile on her face as she got to her feet.

"You've won nothing," Bulat said, and his voice sounded strained even to him. Damn her anyway for sticking the sword in his back. As long as it was there, he wouldn't heal, and he couldn't reach around to grab it himself.

Alfredo, however, was staring at Bulat angrily. "You were *supposed* to keep her occupied, you big jackass! Now I gotta start *all* over!"

"Were you this whiny when you were Yaga's apprentice," Buffy said, "or is this a new thing?"

"Shut up! You'll be laughin' outta the other side of your mouth when Koschei's resurrected—you *and* that Russian witch!"

Now Buffy looked thoughtful, though Bulat suspected she was being ironic. "Y'know, I've always wondered about that. How *do* you laugh out of the other side of your mouth?"

"I said shut up! Bulat!"

Bulat had to admit he was amused by the exchange, but then he didn't really like Alfredo all that much. As a means to an end—specifically, Bulat's own end—he was useful, but beyond that Bulat preferred to avoid the bald, ugly fool. Indeed, he had seized on the notion of insinuating himself into the Slayer's camp and spying on Baba Yaga in part because it got him away from Alfredo and his constant complaints.

Still, Alfredo had a point. Bulat was supposed to distract Buffy while Alfredo completed the *Vozrozhdeniye*. Lifting his sword gingerly, he moved toward the Slayer.

She moved faster, though, kicking him without even looking first, her heel colliding with his stomach. He stumbled backward as air pushed out of his mouth.

The cold sensation of metal in his back suddenly intensified—and then went away.

The Slayer's kick hadn't just knocked the air out of him, it had knocked the sword out as well. Bulat smiled and started to regain his footing, preparing to impale this tiresome Slayer once and for all.

But then she kicked him *again,* sending him reeling backward into one of the crates. Splinters from the wood cut into his back where he'd been wounded and hadn't yet healed, sending pain shooting along his entire spine. He fought past it. He'd had quite enough of this.

Buffy bent over and picked up the sword that had been in Bulat's back. Her second kick had sent him far enough away from her weapon that she could rearm herself.

"I have toyed with you enough, Slayer, okay? Now we play for keeps."

A smile that disconcerted Bulat more than he was willing to admit spread across Buffy's face. "Only way to play, Bulat."

He thrust forward with his sword, and she effortlessly parried. With a shock Bulat realized that the strength of his strike was nowhere near what it should have been. *This girl has weakened me.* Part of him was grateful—this would, after all, be his last battle. *Only fitting that it be a fine one.*

His own lips sliding back into a smile, he went for her head, then swung down quickly to her hip. She parried both blows, unsurprisingly, since it was a fairly standard tactic. He then switched hands and swirled around toward Buffy's neck; she barely managed to duck the blade. Bulat pressed his advantage and swung toward her chest on the other side.

She parried that—easily. No one had done so in almost a hundred years. But even as he parried the Slayer's own attack, Bulat realized he was striking with considerably less speed than his usual. His back was also starting to grow numb. *I don't understand, I usually can heal much faster—*

And then it hit him—so hard that he almost forgot to block another of Buffy's thrusts—that with the *Vozrozhdeniye* begun, Bulat might no longer be immortal.

Good, he thought as he pressed forward, trying to keep the Slayer off balance. *Then all I have to do is delay this girl for a little while longer.*

Even as they continued to thrust and parry, Bulat began to wonder where the other Slayer was. . . .

Oz was concerned.

He wasn't nervous. That wasn't really his thing. For one thing, nerves used up a lot of energy, and Oz preferred to use as little energy as possible. He wasn't sure what he was saving it for, but he figured he'd need it in spades when he did, so best to save it all up. There were those who said that this dearth of energy contributed to his somewhat lackluster guitar play, and Oz wasn't likely to argue the point.

"Is everything gonna be okay?" Michael, who was seated next to him in the passenger seat of his van, asked.

"Usually."

Michael was actually twiddling his thumbs, something Oz had never seen anyone do in real life before. As a general rule, Michael subscribed to the Goth ethic of studied disinterest, of which Oz generally approved, but this was a little out of his normal range. "What's that mean?" Michael asked, sounding a bit worried.

"I mean that Buffy usually pulls some kind of rabbit out of her hat. Not a real rabbit," he added, in case Michael was confused.

"No, I get that. It's funny, I said that I'd cast the spell, but I gotta tell ya—I'm *real* glad I didn't have to. I mean, I've cast a few protections and a glamor or two when I had a date, but this—this is some serious stuff. I knew Willow was getting into the hardcore magicks, but I had no idea."

"It's definitely serious," Oz said. He might have said more—though that was pretty unlikely, all things considered—but he noticed something out of the corner of his eye. He peered out the windshield to get a better look.

Something was approaching over the horizon. It seemed to be three people flying through the air.

Michael followed Oz's gaze. "What the heck is that?"

Oz just shook his head, then grabbed the crossbow from near his feet and opened the driver's side door in the hopes of getting a better look. He recognized Willow's scent before he was able to make out her face, and a sense of relief washed over him, so much so that he changed his facial expression slightly. He also put the crossbow back in the van.

The three figures—Oz assumed the other two to be Baba Yaga and Faith, though they were still too far away to make out—were very close together and standing upright, which Oz thought was odd for people flying through the air. He had always assumed that people with the power of flight would fly akin to the way Superman did; if nothing else, it was more aerodynamic. They were also staying close to the rooftops.

When the trio got closer, Oz was able to make out the faces of the Russian sorceress, Slayer Mark II, and the love of his life. He also realized why they were standing upright and staying so close together: They weren't flying, the thing they were standing in was flying.

"Is that a bowl?" Michael had also gotten out of the van, and now stood with his mouth hanging open.

"A mortar. Willow said that Baba Yaga used to fly around in one of those—she steers with the pestle."

"That's just weird."

Pausing to reflect on the irony of a Goth warlock commenting to a werewolf while in the proximity of two sorceresses, two Slayers, a former Watcher, and a vampire with a soul about what might be considered weird, Oz then stepped in front of the van, where Michael joined him. The mortar came in for a landing right next to them. Oz noticed that Willow was holding a bell jar that held a big, bloodshot blue eye suspended in water. He figured this was the infamous Eye of Argon.

Grinning ear to ear, Willow sang, "Here we come to save the *day*!" as she stepped out of the mortar.

Oz raised an eyebrow. "Never figured you for a Mighty Mouse fan."

"I am full of layers and depths. Like an onion."

Yaga looked tense as she said, "And like an onion, you are making me weep. Has the *Vozrozhdeniye* begun?"

Nodding, Oz said, "Buffy, Angel, and Giles are trying to delay things. Not sure how they're doing, but Angel jumped through the skylight about ten minutes ago."

"That usually means heroism's on the agenda," Willow said.

Faith looked like a coil about to spring. "Fine, let's go kick some ass."

Yaga smirked. "Ah, good."

"What?" Faith asked.

"While a great deal of metal and other nonorganic products stand between us and the ritual, there is also quite a bit of paper and wood."

"I don't get it," Oz said with a frown.

Willow said, "Baba Yaga can control dead things."

"And paper and wood are dead trees." Oz nodded. "Got it."

For her part, Yaga closed her eyes and started muttering something.

Suddenly, with a resounding crack and crash that actually hurt Oz's eardrums for a moment, the near wall of the warehouse ripped apart, like a giant, invisible hand had grabbed the wall at its center and torn it in two like a piece of paper. Sparks flew, as Yaga's rending of the wall probably ripped out some wiring.

"Um, wow," said Willow, whose eyes had gone all

wide again—something Oz had always found adorable, along with all of her other facial expressions. "I didn't know you could do that."

Yaga stepped forward. "I could not a second time, I fear."

"You don't gotta," Faith said, running forward. "Let's move!"

Peering into the giant hole in the wall Yaga had made, Oz saw a rather scary tableau. There was a big circle of people. Oz couldn't see what was inside the circle, but Angel was hovering motionless above it. Off to the side, he saw Buffy engaged in a pretty impressive sword fight with Bulat the Brave. *Coulda sworn he was on our side,* Oz thought. Of Giles there was no sign.

Yaga turned to Oz as Faith ran toward where Bulat and Buffy were fighting. "Mr. Osborne, you said that Angel went through the skylight ten minutes ago?"

Shrugging, Oz said, "Give or take."

"The *Vozrozhdeniye* only began a few minutes ago." Yaga smiled. "Excellent. Ms. Summers must have disrupted the spell and forced Alfredo to begin anew. We are fortunate. Come, Willow."

Trying very hard not to think about the fact that Yaga now felt comfortable calling Willow by her first name, Oz said, "What can we do?"

"Mr. Czajak may aid us by joining the circle. As you Americans put it, every little bit helps." She produced a stick of chalk. "You may assist, Mr. Osborne, by drawing a circle. It must be large enough for the three of us to sit in."

Taking the chalk and giving Willow an encouraging look, he said, "One circle, comin' up."

Before he could start, he whirled around. "Smoke."

"I smell nothing," Yaga said.

With a tap of the body part in question, Oz said, "The nose knows. How fast is the counterspell?"

"It will have to be fast enough," Yaga said grimly.

Chapter Sixteen

Buffy's shoulders were aching, her arms felt like two pieces of wet spaghetti, her heart was pounding at three times its usual speed, sweat was pouring down into her eyes, and her legs felt like two lead weights attached to her hips.

But at least I'm not dead. Bulat was as good with a sword as anyone she'd seen or faced, and the only reason Buffy was keeping ahead was because he was also incredibly slow. Buffy assumed that it was her own Slayer-induced speed, combined with her stabbing him literally in the back the way he'd stabbed her metaphorically, that provided the advantage, but whatever it was, she'd take it.

Suddenly, the wall and several crates split apart like the Red Sea when Moses was done with it, and both Bulat and Buffy looked over in surprise at their sudden view of the parking lot. Buffy took half a second to see that Faith, Willow, and Yaga were with Oz and Michael outside, then turned her attention back to Bulat—which was good, as he had recovered faster and gone for her head.

Two more parries, and then Buffy heard someone running toward them.

"You up for a threesome there, B?"

"The more, the merrier," Buffy said as she parried another thrust to her neck.

Bulat then whirled around and swung at Faith's head. She ducked and rolled, coming up on her left side, bracing herself on the floor with her hands and left leg, and kicking up right into Bulat's stomach with her right foot.

Taking advantage of the opportunity, Buffy swung her sword at Bulat, intending to cut his stomach open.

But Faith's kick took him down farther than she'd expected, and the sword instead sliced clean through his neck.

Bulat's body fell to the ground with a thud, as his head started rolling like a bowling ball toward one of the boxes.

Buffy just stood there, openmouthed. "Okay, I wasn't planning on doing that. I just wanted to hurt him, not kill him."

The head collided with a box and came to a stop, face up. Bulat's eyes stared lifelessly at the ceiling.

Then the eyes blinked.

Not so lifelessly, Buffy thought, as the disembodied head spoke: "That was—unexpected."

Faith stood up next to Buffy. "How immortal *is* this guy?"

All at once, the ground started to shake. "I think we're about to find out."

I'll show her. I'll show them all.

That had been the primary thought in Alfredo LaManna's mind ever since that bitch had kicked him out seven years ago.

Okay, so he blew up the parking garage. Like she hadn't done worse in her time. Bulat still recalled reading in her own library about how she had let someone trick her into doing a favor, one that resulted in the death of an entire royal family, just because she underestimated someone's ability to tame her horses. With the royals' death, the demesne fell into chaos, and it was all Yaga's fault. That was a lot worse than blowing up some stupid garage. There was nobody *in* the garage except for one attendant, and he just sustained a few burns and scrapes, so the only damage was to the cars, and insurance probably covered that mostly.

But, no, one garage goes boom, and it's out the door, Alfredo. *Well, fine. I'll show you just what I could've been if you'd believed in me, you bitch.*

He'd learned a lot more on his own than the oh-so-famous Baba Yaga could possibly have taught him anyhow. Neither she nor any other necromancer could affect the immortality spell or whoever it was cast on, but Alfredo had found a way around it in the rare books room of that small research library in Vancouver. The librarians wouldn't let him copy the text, the bastards, so he had to steal it—which had proved harder than he'd thought, thanks to the damned newfangled bar code system. Eventually, though, he managed it, and had the text.

Finding Bulat had been the masterstroke of luck. It was the perfect match, as both of them wanted Koschei back *and* they both wanted the bitch goddess from hell to suffer.

And Alfredo knew that Koschei would make Yaga suffer. After all, from what he'd read, the Deathless was not one to forgive the person responsible for making that title a lie.

Of course, now that it was happening, there were all these *setbacks,* mostly because of Bulat. *He may have lived for a few centuries, but he's accumulated, like,* no *wisdom in that time.* For starters, "the Brave" was supposed to keep this town's two Slayers off Alfredo's back, and he couldn't even do *that* right. Here he was, trying to cast a resurrection in peace, and the blond Slayer and her pet vampire were screwing with the program.

The setbacks were not all Bulat's fault. Having to deal with that little weasel of a principal just to get the damned ring contract was like getting teeth pulled without the Novocaine. It had taken all the money he'd saved up and stolen over the years in order to finance the ring operation, but it was worth it. After all, the stars were aligned for the *Vozrozhdeniye* right at the same time Sunnydale High's students were getting their class rings. It was fate, dropping all the souls he'd need right into his lap!

And then there was the matter of getting his hands on the warehouse, which had a whole bunch of other red tape attached to it. Bulat was no help, since apparently they didn't have bureaucracy in tsarist Russia. Or if they did, he'd avoided it. *Probably just killed anyone who got in his way.*

If Bulat can just hold the Slayer off for a few more minutes . . . The corpse Bulat had stolen was twitching again, and the life essence of the students continued to pour into it. *Soon, soon!*

Then the wall and a bunch of the crates ripped apart.

This can't be good. Alfredo, however, refused to let it distract him, even though he figured it had to be Yaga, which meant that Bulat had screwed up *again. If I live through this, I'm going to kill him, immortality be damned.*

When the ground started to shake, Alfredo got really worried. He concentrated harder, continuing to mutter the Russian words he'd been chanting for the last half hour, trying to do as Yaga had taught him, *willing* the magic to work.

The corpse stopped twitching. Something was wrong.

Alfredo could feel the soul essence of the students start to go in reverse, like a tape being rewound. *Oh no you don't!* Instead of muttering the chant, he shouted the words to the *Vozrozhdeniye,* screaming at the top of his lungs.

I won't let you beat me again, you bitch!

He hadn't expected a response, but then Yaga's voice

sounded in his head: *"Of course you will, young fool. You are nothing to me, and I'm about to show you why."*

One of the walls caught fire, and the flames spread with appalling speed. Alfredo could feel the heat of the flames warming his entire right side.

When he felt the life essences of the students moving faster, back into their proper places, Alfredo screamed.

Willow concentrated.

She'd been practicing this spell for a week now, and she was pretty sure her pronunciation was right, even with all the *y* sounds. Next to her, Michael was concentrating also, but not chanting, as he hadn't learned the spell's words. Still, he knew how to channel mystical energy just fine, and that was a big help.

Usually, when Willow cast spells, she felt a warm glowy kind of sensation all through her bones. It was nice and tingly, like a shower with fresh soap. Necromancy, though, was nothing like that. For starters, there was the serious stinky factor. And instead of being warm and glowy, it was dark and cold, the way it felt after walking in the rain for hours.

But she continued to chant alongside Baba Yaga, knowing that what they did may have been icky as all get-out, but if she didn't, her classmates would die.

To save innocent lives, she could bear a little ick.

Suddenly, the cold grew worse. Baba Yaga's chanting became louder, and she could hear someone screaming words in Russian from inside the warehouse. *That's probably Alfredo.*

Her heart started to feel weird, and she began to have trouble breathing. Baba Yaga's voice sounded in Willow's head, even as the sorceress's mouth continued to speak the counterspell, but her telepathy was weak: *"He is resisting us! The counterspell is not working!"*

Willow opened her eyes. She could hear Alfredo chanting the *Vozrozhdeniye* at the top of his lungs. She saw Oz, standing outside the circle. And she saw Xander, along with the other seniors, his soul being drained.

Not if I can help it. He's not getting away with giving Xander an evil ring! She gathered every fiber of her soul, called upon the tingly feeling of the magic she was accustomed to, and pushed it into the cold and dark, augmenting it, making it brighter.

Alfredo shouted, but now it was a full-throated scream: "No! No, no, no, *noooooooooooooooooooo*!"

Baba Yaga's voice was now resounding in Willow's mind: *"Yes, yes, and yes, my former pupil."*

Everything went white in a spectacular glow.

Lesley Anton found herself standing by her kitchen table. The house was dark.

She frowned. The last thing she remembered was finishing off her orange juice after putting the Cheerios bowl and spoon in the sink. But that had happened first thing in the morning, and now it was dark out. And Mother had disappeared.

Glancing over at the microwave, she saw that it was 8:24, which meant that Mother was still at work, and somehow Lesley had lost the entire day.

Her right ring finger felt funny. Reaching down, she grabbed the ring to take it off, but it shocked her with a small jolt of static electricity. Yanking her left hand back and shaking off the shock, she held up her right hand to stare at it.

God, what an ugly ring.

She grabbed it again, this time managing to touch it without causing sparks, and looked more closely at it.

That's weird. The company logo's gone.

Lesley went up to her room and put the ring in a drawer. *I hate this stupid town. I so can't wait to graduate so I can move to La Jolla.* She'd been accepted to the University of California–San Diego, and she planned to move into her off-campus apartment with her two girlfriends the day after graduation. In fact, after this crap, she was seriously considering skipping graduation. She'd talk with Shari and Danni about it today—or, rather, tomorrow, since today seemed to have disappeared.

Oddly, considering she just finished her breakfast, she was hungry. *Of course, that was hours ago. I wonder what happened* this *time? God, I* hate *this stupid town!*

She went back to the kitchen to see what frozen goodness awaited her in the freezer.

Cordelia Chase was suddenly standing at her front door.

"Miss Chase? You okay?" Lupe said, coming down the stairs. "Finally home from school? It's eight thirty, you know, and I was worried. Oh, and there was someone who came by earlier to see you."

Blinking in confusion, Cordelia asked, "What?" How could it be eight thirty? Why was it dark?

She started to walk toward Lupe, and stumbled. Picking up her left foot, she saw that the heel of her shoe was missing. "I don't believe this! These are three-hundred-dollar pumps! Ruined!"

Lupe just ignored her and continued. "She was all small and blond—"

"Wait a minute, small and blond?"

"Yes."

It figures. Something crazy happens, and Buffy the Vapid Slayer's right in the middle of it. "I bet there's some kind of shoe-eating demon out there possessing people, and Buffy *better* get to the bottom of it, because I'm *not* losing anymore footwear, I can tell you *that*."

Percy West and Hogan Martin materialized in Percy's driveway. Hogan was sitting on the ground, with Percy standing nearby.

"Dude, where's my car?" Hogan asked.

Percy looked up. "Dude, where's the sun?" He looked at his watch. "Eight thirty. That *can't* be right."

Hogan, however, was focused on his ride. He got to his feet and looked down the avenue. "We have *got* to find my car. Dad hasn't finished paying it off yet. He'll *kill* me."

"Relax, dude," Percy said, "we'll find it. It probably went to the same place the sun went. We find who took the sun, we'll find your Chevy."

"How does your brain form speech? I mean, seriously, dude, nobody *stole* the sun. We just lost the day, okay? And somebody took my car."

"C'mon, it's just a Chevy. Who'd steal that?"

"Whatever, dude, we gotta find it." Hogan slapped Percy's chest with the back of his hand and started walking down the street. "C'mon, let's go."

Rolling his eyes, Percy followed.

"Hey, you hungry?"

Harmony Kendall stood in the driveway of her own house. Her car was nowhere to be found, and it was dark.

"Okay, *what's* going on?"

"Harmony!"

She turned around to see her mother running out the door.

"Mom?"

Mom immediately grabbed her and hugged her hard. "Oh, my baby! I'm so glad you're okay!"

"Uh, *duh*, Mom, of course I'm okay. But where's my car? And why is it nighttime?"

Refusing to let go, Mom said, "You've been missing all day, dear, and I was *so* worried!" Then, finally, she broke her deathgrip on Harmony. "Come inside, I'll fix you some dinner."

"O-okay. I'm actually kinda hungry." Harmony didn't get what was going on, then decided it wasn't worth thinking about. If Mom was okay, then so was everything else. It was probably one of those weird things Buffy and her friends were always involved in.

Cordelia would tell her *all* about it tomorrow.

For now, though, she'd have dinner with Mom, which would be *awful*, but at least there'd be food. She really was hungry, like she hadn't eaten all day. . . .

Xander Harris was all of a sudden looking at the front door of his house.

Great. I got possessed. Again.

He immediately walked out the door before either of his parents could notice his sudden appearance. Going straight for Uncle Rory's car, he leapt over the convertible's driver's side door with the intent of sliding gracefully into the seat and slamming the keys into the ignition. That plan was somewhat ruined by his right sneaker catching on the window, and he collapsed into the car in a tangle of limbs.

Sighing, he extricated himself and remembered that he hadn't actually taken the keys out of his pocket, which would've screwed up the maneuver even if he hadn't been such a klutz.

Reaching into his pocket for the keys, he thought, *It always has to be me, doesn't it? I'm the one who gets seduced by the praying mantis, I fall for the killer mummy girl, I get possessed by the hyena spirit, I fall for the BGOC—which in this case stands for Bitch Girl on Campus—I get recruited by the zombie gang from hell. Why is it always me?*

Then, as he put the convertible in gear, he remembered that he'd also saved Buffy's life and gotten to have sex with Faith. *So it's not all bad.*

Either way, when bad stuff was going down in Sunnydale, Xander's first stop was the library. So that was where he steered Uncle Rory's car, determined to do whatever he could to help Buffy save the world. Again.

Buffy blinked the spots out of her eyes after the blinding flash of light and realized three things at once:

The first was that the seniors had all disappeared, meaning, if nothing else, that Buffy would be spared from having to save their butts and explain what happened to all of them. She just hoped that Yaga's counterspell hadn't killed them all. *If it did, no protection spell in the world is gonna save her.*

The second was that Angel had fallen on top of Alfredo, an image Buffy planned to amuse herself with later when she had time.

And third, and of most immediate importance, the warehouse was on fire.

Next to her, Faith said, "Okay, *that* was wicked cool."

"Giles!" She turned and ran back toward the entrance where she had come in, yelling back to the other Slayer as she did so. "Faith, get everyone outta here!"

Without bothering to see if Faith complied, Buffy ran back to where she thought she remembered Giles being. She had run around being chased by Bulat for so long that she wasn't sure which way was up anymore—especially after Yaga had ripped the warehouse in half.

After what seemed like forever, she found him, not by sight, but by the sound of British groaning.

"Giles!" She followed the moan to the prone form of a tall man struggling to rise.

"My head." He looked up at Buffy, and she couldn't help but splutter a laugh when she saw his glasses were balanced cockeyed on his nose. "Buffy?"

"Sorry, Giles, but we need to get outta here. Place is burning."

"The *Vozroz*—"

Tossing her sword to her left hand, she grabbed Giles's elbow with her right and started pulling him up—no mean feat, even with Slayer strength, as right now Giles was tweed-clad dead weight. "Worry not, the *Vozrozh* has all been *deniye*'d. But the warehouse is on fire, so we need to vamoose."

"Of course." Giles pulled himself upright the rest of the way, gave Buffy a grateful smile, and then they headed back the way Buffy had come.

Just as she got to the circle where the *Vozrozh-deniye* was being performed, she saw Alfredo and Angel struggling. Angel was down on his knees, sweat beading on his distended brow. He had his game face on, and it looked like Alfredo was trying to put some kind of magical whammy on him.

Hoisting the sword and holding it like a spear, Buffy threw it at Alfredo.

It went sailing past his head and into one of the boxes. *Now I know why Giles never trained me in swordthrowing.*

However, it distracted Alfredo for a second, allowing Angel to haul off and belt him hard enough to send him skidding across the floor.

Alfredo rose surprisingly quickly, then grabbed something off the floor and ran outside.

"Oh no you don't," Buffy muttered, and she ran after him. She could hear only one set of footfalls behind her, which she presumed to be Angel's. Giles was in no shape for a fight, anyhow.

However, when she and Angel got out to the parking lot, she saw Alfredo and Bulat's head—which, she realized, was what Alfredo had picked up—suspended in midair. On the other side of them were Yaga, with her hands raised, as well as Faith, Oz, Michael, and Willow, all standing around Oz's van. Buffy also saw what looked like a big bowl next to the van, and also a big circle that had been drawn in chalk on the pavement. Several charred herbs and a big bell jar containing a gross eye were in the center of that circle. Buffy figured the latter was the infamous Eye of Argon.

Yaga asked, "Did you truly think you would get away that easily—either of you?"

It was Bulat who replied. "I had my hopes, Grandmother. Please, you must kill me."

Smiling that annoying smile, Yaga said, "Now why would I do that, young Bulat? After all, it is your fondest wish, and you have given me no reason to grant any of your wishes."

"I cannot live like this!"

"Oh, you can—you simply cannot live comfortably."

"Where's Giles?" Willow asked.

As if to add urgency to Willow's already frantic question, the fire spread to the entire warehouse, which went up in flames with a giant *foomph*. Buffy whirled around, intending to run in after Giles, when the ex-Watcher came dashing out on his own, holding the sword in one hand, a handkerchief wrapped around the hilt.

When he caught up to Buffy, looking a lot more winded than he should have from such a brief jog, Buffy grinned. "You just *had* to get the sword, didn't you?"

He managed a smile back, though it was a ragged one. "It actually belongs to the Council. I fully intend to tell *them* that it was lost in the fire, but I rather like the weight of it."

Yaga then said, "I suggest we retire from the scene posthaste." In the background, Buffy heard the wail of sirens, indicating the impending arrival of the firefighters, not to mention Sunnydale's not-so-finest.

"Back to the library, I think," Giles said. Then he looked around the parking lot. "Er, Faith? What have you done with my car?"

Epilogue

Buffy was incredibly relieved to see Xander waiting for them at the library—along with Cordelia. Xander looked equally relieved to see them, especially since it had sounded like he and Cordy had been yelling at each other before Buffy and the others had arrived. They had all ridden over together in Oz's van, save for Yaga, Alfredo, and Bulat's head. *They* had ridden in Yaga's mortar.

Willow was the first to give Xander a big hug, quickly followed by Buffy. Oz, Michael, and Giles settled for handshakes, and Faith and Xander just exchanged a weird look. Feeling the milk of human kindness after their successful battle, Buffy even hugged Cordelia.

"It was weird," Xander said. "Last thing I remember was leaving for school, and then suddenly I'm in the same place and over twelve hours have passed. I figure I was possessed—*again*."

"Er, after a fashion," Giles said. He was emerging from his office, pressing an ice pack against the back of his head.

Cordy said, "All I know is, I was eating breakfast, and suddenly I lost half the day. And my *heel* broke. I figured it was some kind of shoe-eating demon, so I came here to see if you'd stop it for me." She reached into her purse and took out a pump that was missing its heel. "I even brought the shoe, in case you needed it."

"It was your class rings, actually," Giles said, and then he explained what had happened.

Xander held up his hand and looked at it as if it were diseased. "You mean I worked my *tuchus* off hauling boxes for a month so I could get possessed? *Again?*" Yanking the ring off and tossing it across the room, he said, "I can tell you this—never again. Nuh-uh."

Patiently, Giles said, "Xander, the ring has been neutralized by Baba Yaga's counterspell. It's quite harmless now."

"Wait a minute," Cordelia said. "This can't be right. Willow, didn't you say you can't do magic with gold?"

Willow nodded.

"Then I *couldn't* have been possessed! It had to have been the shoe demon!" She held up her pump for emphasis.

Michael shook his head. "The ring's gold-plated, Cordy. It's really silver. I went with gold too." He showed her his ring, complete with the chip.

Cordelia's eyes widened. "What? Do you know what I *paid* for my ring?"

Nodding, Michael said, "Same as me."

"I do *not* believe this! I'm gonna get a refund if it's the last thing I do!"

Remembering the abandoned offices of Avanas'ev Jewelry, Buffy chuckled and said, "Lotsa luck with that one, Cordy."

Willow looked around. "Uh, shouldn't Yaga be here by now?"

"I'm afraid not, Willow."

"Whoa!" Cordelia cried, backing up and dropping her heel-less shoe. "What is *that*?"

"Baba Yaga communicating telepathically," Giles said. "Why aren't you here?" he then asked.

"I do not see the point. I made Ms. Summers a promise when this all began—that once the time for the Vozrozhdeniye had passed, you would not see me again. I intend to fulfill that promise."

"Uh-huh," Faith said, sounding as dubious as Buffy felt.

"Willow, we all owe you a debt of thanks."

"We do?" Willow asked, her eyes wide with surprise. "Uh, why?"

"Alfredo was more powerful than I had believed. Had I cast the spell alone, he would have been able to resist me. But adding your power—and that of Mr. Czajak—to mine was what made the difference. Your contribution in particular—you have tremendous potential. I'm almost tempted to make another offer to

you as my apprentice, but I know you will not accept."

"What about Bulat and Alfredo?" Buffy asked.

"Worry not, Ms. Summers. I shall deal with my erstwhile apprentice and young Bulat—or at least his head, since the fire has consumed his body—in my own way."

Buffy wasn't sure she liked the sound of that. "Giles, we can't just let her—"

"I welcome you to try to stop me, Slayer. Farewell."

Unwilling to leave it at that, Buffy finished her sentence: "—get away with that!"

Removing the ice pack, Giles said in a gentle voice, "I do not believe we have much choice. Besides, what human jail could hold a sorcerer of even Alfredo's power?"

Angel added, "He's not on Yaga's level, but he almost was able to take possession of me."

"Figures," Xander muttered. "*He* can resist possession."

Oz raised an eyebrow. "You're really having issues with the whole possession thing, aren't you?"

Shaking her head, Willow said, "He's not having issues, he's having subscriptions."

"In *any* case," Angel said, cutting off Xander's attempt to reply, "he's powerful enough that he'd be out of prison in less than a day. Besides, what do you charge him with? Necromancy?"

Cordelia held up her right hand. "Oh, I don't know—fraud, maybe? I paid for a *gold* ring."

Buffy sighed. "And now for a sentence I never

thought I'd say out loud: Cordelia's got a point. Alfredo kidnapped a bunch of seniors and sold rings under false pretenses. There's got to be *something* we can do."

"Still brings us back to the 'jailing him' problem," Angel said.

Shaking her head and holding up her hands, Buffy said, "Fine, but either way, I want to finish things with Ms. Dryanushkina."

"I'm with B," Faith said. "Something about that lady doesn't sit right." Then she smiled. "'Sides, we gotta go back to Chicken-leg Mansion anyhow. I kinda left Giles's car there."

"Yes." Even with the cranial trauma, Giles was able to put the full weight of his prim and proper pissed-offness into that word.

"You guys mind finding alternate transport?" Oz asked. "I want to track down the other Dingoes who got possessed and make sure they're okay."

"I can be Wheel Guy," Xander said. "I've still got the Rorymobile."

Cordelia gave him one of her nastier looks. "I'm stunned you're not out using it to pick up more blond sluts."

Buffy wondered what she was talking about, then decided she *really* didn't want to know. Besides, Xander would probably tell her eventually. He always did.

"By all means, then," Giles said.

"I'll pass too," Angel said.

Buffy had expected as much, especially after the bark-like-a-dog incident that she intended never to reveal to Angel.

He gave her a long, significant look.

Suddenly, Buffy's insides turned to jelly. More than anything else, she wanted to go with him back to the mansion and just *be* with him until—

Until what? He's sufficiently happy and content with life that he turns evil again? Good plan, Buffy.

She looked down and away from him, unwilling to pit her willpower against his eyes.

When she looked up again, he was gone.

Looking at Xander, she said, "Let's go."

Michael also declined to come along, saying he'd had enough excitement for one lifetime, and headed to his own car to drive home. Cordy went to her car without even saying goodbye. Oz and Willow said a slower-than-Buffy-would-have-liked farewell, which involved a lot of kissing. Buffy supposed she would have been more amenable to it if she had someone of her own to kiss.

Buffy, Giles, Willow, and Faith joined Xander in the convertible. Giles, as the tallest, rode shotgun, with the three girls in the back.

"This car *definitely* works better with only two passengers," Faith said.

At that, Buffy shot Faith a look. "How would you know?"

"Didn't X tell you?"

Looking at the driver's side and wishing she could see Xander's face, Buffy said, "No, 'X' didn't."

"He rescued me from some of those Jhe bitches, gave me a lift home."

"It was no big deal," Xander said.

The rest of the ride was relatively silent, until they neared the corner of Palombo. When she saw it, Buffy's heart sank.

It looked almost exactly like the vacant lot Willow had called up on the newspaper website. The only difference was that Giles's Citroën was in the middle of it, with a few dents in the front.

"Buffy," Willow said, "I'm not feeling anything. The illusion spell's gone."

With a glare at Faith, Giles exited Xander's car and headed for his own. Buffy shot Faith a look, and she just shrugged. "Had to get past the freak in skeleton armor somehow."

Willow said, "She had to fight a Forbrat demon, too."

"Nice job," Buffy said. She hadn't actually faced any Forbrat demons, but she'd read up on them during one of many research sessions, and they didn't look like any fun, especially since they could fly.

With a cheeky smile, Faith said, "Thanks, B."

They all hopped out of the convertible and looked at the vacant lot. Giles got into his car and tried the engine, and—to the relief of Buffy, if not Faith, who seemed indifferent—it started without a hitch.

Of the house on chicken legs, there was no sign.

"Bulat said she couldn't be trusted," Buffy said, "but she *did* say we wouldn't see her again. Guess she meant it."

"It's not like Bulat was Mr. Trusty Guy," Willow said.

"Yeah."

Giles backed his car out of the lot, came off the sidewalk with a disturbing *thunk*, and then backed into the road in front of the Rorymobile. Leaning his head out the window, he said, "If you'll all excuse me, I need to return home and consume my entire analgesic supply. Good night."

With a final glare at Faith, he pulled out.

"Now what?" Faith asked.

"I don't know about you guys," Xander said, "but I'm starved. Anybody up for some din-din?"

"Sounds good to me," Buffy said.

"I'm in," Willow added.

Faith grinned. "What the hell. But this time, I call shotgun."

"Great," Xander said. "Let's head to Cluck-o-Rama. I'm in the mood for chicken."

ABOUT THE AUTHOR

Keith R. A. DeCandido also wrote the Buffy novels *The Xander Years, Vol. 1* (1999) and *Blackout* (2006), worked on *The Watcher's Guide, Vol. 1* (with Christopher Golden and Nancy Holder) in 1998, and novelized Joss Whedon's *Serenity* in 2005. In addition, Keith has written novels, novellas, e-books, short stories, comic books, and nonfiction in the media universes of *Star Trek*, *World of Warcraft*, *StarCraft*, *Doctor Who*, Marvel Comics, *Resident Evil*, *Gene Roddenberry's Andromeda*, *Farscape*, *Xena*, and a whole bunch more. Look for the following in 2007: *The Mirror-Scaled Serpent*, the *Voyager* portion of Star Trek: Mirror Universe Book 2: *Obsidian Alliances*; *Command and Conquer: Tiberium Wars*; *Supernatural: Nevermore*; *Star Trek: The Next Generation: Q&A*; and the novelization of *Resident Evil: Extinction*. A student of *Kenshikai* karate, Keith also plays percussion with the parody band the Boogie Knights (www.boogie-knights.org). He lives in the Bronx with his fiancée and their two insane cats. Find out less about Keith at his website, www.DeCandido.net, or follow his ramblings at kradical.livejournal.com.